TWICE ROUND
THE CLOCK

TWICE
ROUND
THE CLOCK

BILLIE HOUSTON

With an Introduction by
Martin Edwards

Poisoned Pen
PRESS

Introduction © 2023, 2024 by Martin Edwards
Twice Round the Clock © 1935 by The Estate of Billie Houston
Cover and internal design © 2024 by Sourcebooks
Front cover image © Mary Evans Picture Library

Published by Poisoned Pen Press, an imprint of Sourcebooks,
in association with the British Library
P.O. Box 4410, Naperville, Illinois 60567–4410
(630) 961-3900
sourcebooks.com

Twice Round the Clock was first published in 1935 by
Hutchinson & Co., London, England.

Cataloging-in-Publication Data is on file with the Library of Congress.

Printed and bound in the United States of America.
VP 10 9 8 7 6 5 4 3 2 1

INTRODUCTION

Twice Round the Clock is a long-forgotten mystery by a woman whose life encompassed professional fame and personal tragedy. Although she was once extremely well-known, it was not as a crime writer. When the book was first published by Hutchinson (a company of considerable renown) in 1935, the dust jacket blurb explained:

> *Billie Houston, as one of the Houston Sisters, is already famous, for she and her sister Renée form what is probably the best known and most successful vaudeville sister act within living memory, and there must be few indeed who, through the music-hall and newspapers and wireless, are not acquainted with the smiling, fair-haired "boy."*
>
> *And now Billie Houston has turned novelist and here is her first novel. It is a thriller and a gripping one too. A man is murdered at a dinner party held in honour of his daughter at his lonely house. The telephone wires*

have been damaged, cars tampered with, and for long
hours the guests are cooped together, each aware that
his neighbour may be the murderer. A dramatic, excit-
ing situation which Billie Houston develops to the full.

   How this novel came to be written is in itself a story
which tells of many dressing-rooms all over the country
in which between appearances on the stage, pages were
planned and scribbled and often torn up. It tells, too, of
a life-long ambition and an absorbing interest in crim-
inology, and its success may mean to its author more
than thunderous applause from a packed theatre.

The dust jacket was adorned with pictures of Billie
Houston (and her sister Renée) on the front cover as well as
the back, making it clear that her celebrity status—or "plat-
form," in the jargon of the modern publishing world—was
seen as a crucial marketing advantage. I must admit, however,
that when I acquired a copy (inscribed by Billie to Nancy
Maitland in the year of publication) from the estate of the
late Bob Adey, a true bibliophile, I had never heard of either
Billie or her novel. Research uncovered a great deal of material
about the Houston Sisters, but the book itself has seldom
been discussed.

   The undeniable truth is that sometimes forgotten books
have been forgotten for a very good reason. When I started
reading the novel, I was prepared to be disappointed. To my
delight, however, the storyline proved to be lively and unpre-
tentious. The real disappointment was that Billie Houston
never followed up her debut in the genre.

   A keen and intelligent reader of mysteries, she made the

excellent decision to create a sense of pace and suspense by emphasising the rapid passage of time. The title reflects this approach, and so do the chapter headings. This is a country house mystery, and Billie—whose second husband came from an aristocratic family—had rather more extensive personal experience of life in country houses than many writers of Golden Age detection. In a prologue, a body is discovered, but we then have a long flashback scene in which the tension mounts as it becomes evident that numerous people have good cause to commit a murder. The structure anticipates, in some respects, that of a later—and otherwise very different— novel that has justifiably earned acclaim from aficionados of detective fiction: *Lonely Magdalen* by Henry Wade.

Billie Houston was the stage name of Sarah McMahon Gribbin, born in Shettleston, Glasgow, in 1906. Her parents, James Gribbin and Elizabeth Houston, were music hall performers who had a song and dance act. Her older sister Renée (Caterina Rita Murphy Gribbin, 1902–80) began a stage career in 1912. Four years later, with their parents suffering from ill-health, the two girls began working together as the Houston Sisters. In the 1920s, the pair enjoyed sustained popularity, topping the bill in venues around Britain and filling the London Palladium on numerous occasions. They appeared at a Royal Variety Command performance in the days when performers really did take part as a result of a command, or request, from the King.

Typically, they pretended to be children, with Billie playing a boy. According to Frances Gray's essay in the *Oxford Dictionary of National Biography*, the secret of their success lay in meticulous attention to detail: their sets sometimes included furniture that was scaled-up in size so as to make them look like small children. Gray describes the sisters as "both sharply observational about working-class Scottish life and childhood, and sexually magnetic." Billie became highly skilled as a male impersonator.

The sisters appeared together in a handful of films, including *Happy Days are Here Again* (1936), but the act broke up. As Renée explained in her autobiography *Don't Fence Me In* (1974), this was due to Billie's poor health. Renée went on to enjoy a long screen career, with film credits as varied as Roman Polanski's *Repulsion* and *Cul-de-Sac* as well as *A Town Like Alice* and *Carry on at Your Convenience*. A very informative website devoted to Renée may be found at renéehoustonsite.wordpress.com.

Billie's first marriage (to Bobby Wilton, son of the well-known comedian Rob Wilton) ended in divorce, and in 1938 her second husband, the actor Richard Cowper, died. By melancholy coincidence, he and her first husband both took their own lives. In 1939, she married again, to Paul Wills-Eve, and this marriage lasted until her death from emphysema in 1972. They had two children, Carole and Anton, and I'm indebted to Carole for providing me with fascinating background information about her mother. One favourite anecdote concerns Billie, as a very small girl, interrupting a performance of the stage version of *East Lynne*. When her mother declaimed those famously melodramatic lines: "Gone! Gone! And never called me mother!", Billie cried out to reassure her that she was very much alive and kicking.

After the Second World War, Billie was much less visible in public than her sister. This was due in part to the fact that she found contentment in the domestic life but also due to continuing health problems. During one performance she fell from the stage into the orchestra pit and damaged her back severely, necessitating a major operation. Her husband Paul was a journalist who spent several years as bureau chief of United Press International; as a result, the family was based in Paris, a city Billie loved. Carole, who worked in publishing, and Anton, a journalist, both inherited their parents' literary leanings.

From the early 1950s onwards, Billie was a semi-invalid, but she showed considerable courage in coping with her physical limitations and continued to travel extensively. Always a voracious reader of detective fiction, she was a devotee of female authors such as Sayers, Marsh, and Allingham. She also developed into a formidable chess player, reaching regional championship standard.

At one point, Billie thought about writing another crime novel, tentatively titled *Whatever Happened to Aunt Jane?*, but she never got beyond the stage of writing notes for an outline. Nevertheless, *Twice Round the Clock* evidences a genuine talent for storytelling. To this day, debates persist about whether celebrities who publish fiction have some sort of unfair advantage over fellow authors. The reality, however, is that plenty of celebrities write good novels, and even though some of them produce work that is less impressive, it is folly to underestimate an author simply because he or she is well-known in some other walk of life.

I don't claim that *Twice Round the Clock* is a literary masterpiece, but I'm glad that at long last others have a chance to read the story and form their own views about it. Seven years have passed since I wrote about the book on my blog

"Do You Write Under Your Own Name?" but at the time of writing, I'd never come across anyone who had read it, and until now it has remained in the shadows. A new edition as a British Library Crime Classic will change that, and I hope that others will share my view that this is a book deserving of better than total obscurity. Billie Houston was a modest woman who once said to her daughter that the novel was only published because she was a celebrity. I like to think that she would be thrilled to see it enjoying a new life, more than half a century after her death, solely on its own merits.

Martin Edwards

www.martinedwardsbooks.com

A NOTE FROM THE PUBLISHER

The original novels and short stories reprinted in the British Library Crime Classics series were written and published in a period ranging, for the most part, from the 1890s to the 1960s. Many elements of these stories continue to entertain modern readers; however, in some cases there are also uses of language, instances of stereotyping, and some attitudes expressed by narrators or characters that may not be endorsed by the publishing standards of today. We acknowledge that some elements in the works selected for reprinting may continue to make uncomfortable reading for some of our audience. With this series British Library Publishing and Poisoned Pen Press aim to offer a new readership a chance to read some of the rare books of the British Library's collections in an affordable paperback format, to enjoy their merits, and to look back into the world of the twentieth century as portrayed by its writers. It is not possible to separate these stories from the history of their writing and as such the stories are presented as they were originally published with the inclusion of minor edits made for consistency of style and sense, and with pejorative terms of an extremely offensive nature partly obscured. We welcome feedback from our readers.

BOOK ONE

PROLOGUE

Four a.m.

BILL BRENT MADE HIS WAY SWIFTLY ACROSS THE DARK hall, moving with extraordinary quiet for a man of his size.

Arrived at the door of the room from which, he felt sure, the sounds had come, he felt for the knob and grasped it carefully. Even as he did so his head jerked up and he paused for a moment, every sense alert. The faintest sound from somewhere behind him had disturbed the stillness of the night. But the thunder started again with a low rumble, gradually working up to a crashing crescendo, and Brent turned the knob with a swift twist of the wrist and threw the door open.

A gust of cold air rushed through the open door and something white—a sheet of thin paper—fluttered along the floor towards him.

The thunder, having reached its crescendo, commenced to die away, and Brent strained his ears for any sound from the dark room before him. Came another sudden gust of air, the rustling of paper, and more white sheets danced towards him. Then, without warning the room sprang into blue, vivid life as the lightning flashed, and Brent caught his breath at the momentary glimpse of the figure sprawled across the big table with something white and gleaming sticking up out of its back.

He stepped across the threshold and felt on the wall for the switch, found it, and flooded the room with light. Another moment's pause, his eyes fixed upon the figure at the table, and in three strides he was at its side, bending over it.

The table was in chaotic disorder. Papers covered it and overflowed on to the floor at its side. An inkstand had overturned and the contents had trickled out in blue and red streams; the telephone had fallen to the floor, and lay there amongst two or three open books; pens, letter-rack, an overturned ash-tray, were mixed up in the confusion of the table.

Brent bent over the figure of the man seated in the chair with the head and shoulders fallen across the table, and removed a sheet of paper which had fallen across the face and hidden it.

It was Manning, dead, and with the cause of death sticking up from between his shoulder blades—the white ivory handle of a carving-knife. Whoever had put it there had struck with fierce energy, for the blade was buried to within two inches of the handle.

Brent stepped back from the dead man and looked as he felt upon his cheek another rush of cold air.

The French windows were open, and in one of them the centre pane had been smashed. Brent went to them and stared out into the darkness of the night. He was about to step through them on to the lawn outside, when the thunder and lightning came again—together this time—with deafening crash and blinding flash, and he raised his hand in defence of his eyes. Then came the rain, and such rain as Brent had seen before only in the tropics. It beat down with a thunder of its own upon the trees and the lawn outside; it came into the room, wetting his bare feet as he stood near the windows.

Not the slightest use his trying to go out in this storm. He must wait until it passed before attempting to discover the reason for those sounds he had heard beneath his window, and which had brought him hurrying down.

He pulled the windows to and bolted them, and turned again to the room. As he did so something moving at the far end of the hall, which he could see through the open door, caught his eye; something vaguely white, gliding along in the shadows. In a trice he was through the door and making his way towards the place where he had seen it. The light from the room partially lit up the great space of the hall. Whoever it was seemed to have been coming from the dining-room, the door of which was in the far left-hand corner, and... Yes, there it was again, at the foot of the stairs.

Brent reached the broad stairway in time to see it disappear around the first bend, and was about to start up after it, when someone else—a man in pyjamas and dressing-gown—appeared around the bend, flattening himself against the wall as he did so, to let the figure in white pass.

The second figure came lightly and quickly down the stairs. It was Dr. Henderson, and Brent recognised him with relief.

"Bill?" whispered the doctor.

"That's right, Hendy. Who the devil was that going upstairs?"

"Sh! Not too loud. It's Mrs. Geraint sleep-walking. She does it often. What's up down here? I thought I heard sounds, though in this storm…"

"There's plenty up down here, old boy," replied Brent drily. "Manning's in there, murdered…"

"Manning? Murdered?"

"With a damn great knife stuck in him. Come along and have a look for yourself."

The two hurried back to the lighted room, and the doctor bent over the body while Brent waited.

"Dead all right," said Henderson, straightening himself.

"As mutton," agreed Brent.

Henderson stared about him at the wildly disordered room.

"My God!" he said presently, "what a mess!"

"I found the windows open," explained Brent. "Somebody must have come through them, done this"—he pointed to the knife—"and run for it. I heard a sort of scream, and glass breaking…"

"I heard something of the sort, too; about two minutes ago…"

"That's right. Can't go out in this storm, of course. Pity, too, because whoever did this is out in it. I heard him go, and that scream, Hendy, came from outside the windows. My room's directly over this."

The two men stood in silence for a moment, then Brent said: "Better telephone the police, I suppose."

"Yes…yes…I suppose so. Nothing to be done for Manning. You telephone, will you?"

Brent picked up the instrument from the floor and held the receiver to his ear, rattling the hook of the holder as he did so. More rattling of the hook, and then a puzzled look on Brent's face.

"Line's dead," he said. He tried again, but with no result, and presently he put the telephone down amongst the papers on the table.

"No good," he said shortly. "Either the wire's been cut, or the storm's done it in."

Another ear-splitting crash of thunder shook the house, and the night outside lit up with a blinding flash of lightning.

"Better see about the others," said Brent, raising his voice almost to a shout. "Storm's sure to wake them, and we can't have them in here. Helen, too..."

Henderson nodded, and went to the door, looking back as he reached it. Brent was stooping down to look at something under the dead man's head.

"What is it, Brent?" asked Henderson.

"Nothing," came the reply. "Caught sight of a photograph, that's all. His head's lying on an album; look here."

Henderson came and looked.

"Yes," he said, "an album." He made as if to raise the head and draw the album away, but Brent laid a restraining hand on his sleeve.

"Better not touch anything," he said in his usual gruff, short way. "Police better see it as it is, eh?"

"Yes...yes...of course. The police...to be sure."

They turned to the door, and both men pulled up together with a start of surprise. There in the open doorway, her beautiful face as white as chalk, her great eyes distended with horror as they gazed at the sprawling body of the murdered man, stood Helen Manning.

She swayed gently upon her feet as they stared in dismay, and Bill Brent, darting forward, was just in time to catch her as she toppled forward in a dead faint. Without a word he carried her through the door to the hall outside, and across it.

Henderson followed, switching off the light and closing the door behind him, and as he did so, the clock in the room struck four.

Chapter One

Four p.m. on the Day Before

PRECISELY TWELVE HOURS BEFORE, THE SAME CLOCK in the same room had struck the fourth hour of the previous afternoon.

It had been the only sound to disturb the drowsy stillness of the summer afternoon; for, at the moment, no sound had come from the two men who faced each other across the big writing-table.

One of them, Anthony Fane, had put a question to the other, and was waiting for his reply, every feature of his young face betraying the strain of suspense. His eyes were fixed on the face of the man opposite, and as he gazed at the hawk-like nose, the thin, straight line of the mouth, and the half-closed eyes which, strangely alight, met his across the profusion of papers which littered the table, the unaccountable feeling of uneasiness stirred again within him, and, for the hundredth time, he found himself wondering the same thing.

What was there about this man which was so elusive? What exactly was the strange impression he made, the undefinable effect he had upon one? Was it something in those eyes which were never more than half-open? Or something in the little smile which played about the corners of the tight-lipped mouth; or in those long, tapering fingers which, at times, seemed to move like tentacles with an intelligence of their own; something perhaps in the curious habit he had of stroking his cheek with one long, thin finger; or was it…?

"I see. I see."

Anthony gave a little jump as the other broke the silence.

"Yes, sir," he said. "I—er—what I mean is, Helen and I—I mean to say I came over straight away to see you about it… been meaning to speak for some time… I…"

He lapsed into awkward silence, and the other watched him with his eyes still half-closed, and that little curl of the pursed lips which might have been a smile.

"Curious bird, this old Manning," thought Anthony. "Why the devil can't he say yes or no and have done with it, instead of looking at a chap as if he were something under a microscope? Comes of being a genius, I suppose…"

He pulled himself together and cleared his throat nervously. The old man wasn't helping him at all.

"Well, sir?" he asked at last.

Horace Manning, famous in two continents for his scientific achievements, recluse, and something of a closed book even to those of his acquaintances who liked to think themselves his friends, stroked his cheek with a finger, and raised his sparse eyebrows without opening his eyes any wider.

"So you want to marry Helen?" His voice was smooth, quiet, with just the hint of a rasp in it.

"That's roughly the idea, sir. You see I've known Helen

a long time, and—er—I've got enough money of my own for both of us, and of course when the old man—I mean my guv'nor—dies there'll be more, and...well, there it is."

He lapsed again into awkward silence. Helen's father was certainly the most difficult man to talk to he had ever met. Anthony was getting restive under the unremitting stare of those queer eyes. What the dickens was the old boy staring at him like that for?

"And Helen?"

The young man leaned further forward in his seat.

"Oh, she's all for it, sir. I mean..."

"She is in love with you, eh?"

Anthony blinked. Queer expression for this old bird to use.

"Yes, sir. She says so, anyhow."

"Excellent!"

Anthony jumped to his feet, his eyes alight with excitement.

"Then you agree, sir? You give your consent?"

"Why not?" The ghost of a smile flitted about the thin mouth.

Anthony heaved a great sigh of relief.

"Phew!" He mopped his brow with his handkerchief, and then added, naively: "All that fuss and worry for nothing."

"Worry?"

"Yes, sir. Everybody seemed to think..." He stopped short, and swallowed nervously. The older man, the bitter little smile still playing about his lips, waited for him to finish the sentence, and then prompted him.

"You were saying that everybody thought...?"

"Oh, nothing, sir." Anthony coughed nervously. "Helen... er...everybody kept saying you'd never give your consent."

"And why shouldn't I?"

"That's exactly what I said, sir. Why shouldn't you? After all, a corking girl like Helen's got to get married sometime, hasn't she? I mean to say what I can't understand about it is that she hasn't been snapped up before. Why, dash it all, sir, if I may say so, there must have been dozens of chaps wanting to marry Helen, hundreds of 'em, thousands! When I think of it, sir, I can't sleep at nights thinking what a dashed narrow escape I've had. I shall never get over it, sir; never, and you can bet your Sabbath shirt, sir, that I'm going to sit up late, and jolly well burn the midnight oil thinking up plans to make her happy."

"Excellent! Excellent!"

The thin lips seemed hardly to move as the words came from them in the slow, gentle, rasping voice, and once again the strange uneasiness stirred in the breast of Anthony Fane, and he found it necessary to do some more difficult swallowing. If only the old boy wouldn't keep looking at him like that; if only he'd open his eyes properly!

But, after all, here he was giving his consent, and not only giving it, but calling the arrangement excellent. What more could be wanted? Anthony tugged at his tie, cleared his throat, and prepared to wrestle with his exit.

"Well, sir," he began with a poor imitation of ease, "that's that, then, what? I mean to say, there we are, and all we've got to do now is to skip back to the old homestead and celebrate."

"Celebrate, eh? Yes, of course, you will all want to celebrate, no doubt. They will be waiting for your news, I expect?"

"Yes, sir. As a matter of fact we were all talking about it and quite suddenly, just like that"—Anthony snapped his fingers—"I jumped up and said I'd go and tackle the old—I mean I said I would come straight over and settle it once and for all, and as a matter of fact I've got a bet on with young Fraser—I got fours from him—that I'd bring you back alive. What I mean is that you'd come straight over with me in the old bus and join in the joy. The guv'nor's there, and old Henderson, and Helen's been there all day, as you know, sir, and one or two others, and what with this and that, there'll be some sprightly doings when I take my news back, I shouldn't wonder. What about it, sir? All you've got to do is to step into the old bus at the door, and you'll be there before you know it. She can do sixty when pushed, and when she's decarbonised, she'll touch seventy. Young Fraser's with me, but we can empty him into the dicky. What d'you say, sir?"

Horace Manning got up from his chair and turned his back for a moment upon the young man. Anthony watched him, admiring the straightness of the lean body, and noting the fact that he seemed to move without making a sound; like a cat…

Anthony almost jumped as the other turned slightly and looked at him over his shoulder. One finger was gently massaging the cheek, and the queer little smile seemed to be making an effort to extend itself.

"Suppose you all come and celebrate here?"

"Here, sir?" Astonishment lent Anthony's remark emphasis.

"Why not? If you will convey my compliments to Sir Anthony and Lady Fane, and tell them how glad I will be if they and their guests will give me the pleasure of dining here this evening in celebration of your engagement to my daughter, I will be obliged."

"Of course, that's most awfully splendid, sir. Downright handsome, I call it…" Anthony looked doubtful.

"Quite a proper procedure in the circumstances, eh?"

"Oh, quite, sir, quite! Magnificent idea! I'll go straight back and put it to them…"

"At the same time explaining the shortness of the notice by the suddenness of the event which provides its occasion."

Anthony blinked once or twice. "Quite so," he agreed. "Er—what sort of time? Sevenish, eh?"

"An excellent time! And if you will be able to lend me my daughter for an hour or two before that time…"

"Exactly. Yes, of course."

"Very well, then, we will regard that as settled." Anthony held out his hand, and the older man gave him his—a soft, limp, curiously dry hand, with seemingly no strength in it at all. Anthony could not even grip it heartily.

A moment later Anthony was being shown out of the front door by Strange, the Mannings' butler and Mr. Edward Fraser, who, for his greater comfort while he indulged in a cigarette which was inserted into the end of a foot-long holder, had draped his legs over the side of the low, rakish two-seater, watched his friend give his brow a vigorous mopping as he descended the steps, and augured the worst.

"Never mind, my son," said Mr. Fraser as Anthony walked around the car to the other side and put one foot over. "Bolt with the girl. Do a bunk. Gretna Green. And that'll be four of the best. Pay up and look pleasant, eh?"

Anthony got the rest of himself into the driver's seat, pushed the starter down, and the car shot away down the drive with a suddenness which necessitated violent contortions on the part of Mr. Fraser who had not completed the business of arranging himself in his seat. The car shot through the big gates of "Treeholme" and came to a sudden stop in the road outside. Anthony mopped his brow once more, and then sat back in his seat.

"Of all the queer birds!" he said thoughtfully.

"You mean old Manning, eh? Helen's Pop? Bit cracked, so I've always heard. Loose in the plates. But there you are, that's what comes of being a genius and messing about with test-tubes and things. Never be a genius, my son. Cut it right out if the idea's ever occurred to you. And now tell uncle. Was he awful? Did he boot you round the house, or have you thrown to the canary, or anything like that?"

"Sort of looks at you as if you were something pinned to a board," said Anthony pensively.

"Well, if that's all he did to you…gave you a good look, I don't see what you've got to complain about. What's in a look. I mean a look more or less…"

"But the funny thing about it, Teddy," resumed Anthony as if he had not been interrupted, "is that it's all okay."

"What?"

"It's all over bar the cheers of the crowd and the mounted police, and the photographs in the paper. Joy, in short, may now reign supreme."

"You mean the old turnip has said: 'bless you, my son'?"

"I do an' all."

"Go on!"

"He not only gave his consent, but he said: 'Excellent.' Said it four times. And as for bringing him back alive, we're all going over there tonight to dinner to celebrate. The whole bagful. The complete outfit, and that will be sixteen of the best up your shirt, old cock, and if you can't cough up at once, I don't mind letting it hang over for a bit."

Mr. Fraser removed the holder from his mouth, turned to his companion, and thrust out a hand which the other took and shook in silence.

"Thanks very much, old boy," Anthony said presently, "and regarding the sixteen, take your time, old boy; just jolly well take your time."

Mr. Fraser seized his companion's hand and wrung it again. Then he sat back and surveyed him earnestly.   .

"What's it feel like to be engaged? I should like to know straight from the horse's mouth what I'm going to feel like when I bring Kay up to the scratch."

Anthony's eyes were fixed vacantly upon the little flag which fluttered above the radiator of the car.

"I'll tell you some time, old boy," he said. "I can't get that chap out of my mind somehow. I've been wondering why it was Helen was so upset whenever I talked about going to see him. He's such a queer bird…sort of dashed creepy…" He gave a little shudder in the middle of which the car shot forward again.

And as the car, under the expert hands of Anthony, ate up the fifteen miles which separated Treeholme from Fane Court, the "queer bird" sat at his big writing-table studying an album of photographs. They were mostly of a woman with frightened eyes in a beautiful face. In some of them she had with her a child very like her. And presently there were no more photographs of the woman, only those of the child growing bigger until, at the end of the album she had become a beautiful young girl. He studied the last of them, beneath which was written in small, fine writing: *Helen, 1933.* That was only a year ago—less than that.

He took the photograph out of the page, turned back to the pictures of the woman, and put it alongside one of them. The same frightened eyes, and—almost uncannily—the same face. Yes, Helen was the living image of her mother—even to the unmistakable fear in the eyes.

He closed the book and, placing his elbows on the table, cupped his narrow face in his hands, beating a little tattoo upon his temples with the long, tentacle-like fingers. His eyes closed still more until they were mere slits, and about the almost invisible lips played a tiny smile.

Horace Manning, brilliant scientist, acclaimed genius throughout the civilised world, was indulging in his favourite pastime. He was thinking back to that woman with the frightened eyes; thinking down the years as the child grew up; thinking of the girl now awaiting her lover fifteen miles away…thinking of *her* frightened eyes.

There was only one title which could have been put to a portrait of him as he sat there at half-past four on this close, summer afternoon: "*Cruelty.*"

Chapter Two

Half-Past Four to Half-Past Five

HALF-PAST FOUR TO HALF-PAST FIVE ON THAT SAME afternoon…the time during which everybody in the district began to notice that it was getting very close, very oppressive, very sultry.

Otherwise there was little of outstanding interest about this particular hour, and none of those people who, in the course of a few days, were destined to reply to the Coroner's questions about it, did anything or experienced anything which they could afterwards recall as being of importance, or of any great value to the inquiry.

Mrs. Geraint, who had been housekeeper to the Mannings since Miss Helen was a baby, spent the first part of it wandering about the gardens of Treeholme with a new camera which Miss Helen had given her for her birthday.

Rounding a corner of the house she came suddenly upon Strange, the butler, whom she discovered in the act of helping himself to a pear from the tree which grew against the wall in which were the French windows of the scientist's study. She put her camera up to snap him, and might have got quite a good picture had not Strange suddenly turned and seen her.

Mrs. Geraint caught a fleeting glimpse of the fury which distorted the usually placid face of the man as he sprang at her and struck the camera from her hands, and before she had time to recover from her surprise, there he was on his knees, picking up the camera, seeing that it was not broken, and explaining to her that he was superstitious about having his photograph taken.

Queer! Very queer affair altogether! But then, she had never quite liked that Strange. Too smarmy and deep for her liking, and she was always coming across him slinking down corridors, or just coming from a closed door. Indeed, if it were not for her master, Horace Manning, she would have put him down as the first man she had ever really disliked and mistrusted. But with Manning about, she had no dislike left for anybody else. She did not so much dislike Manning, as hate him. Something about him made her very bones creep, and roused in her a hatred which was deep, instinctive, and almost violent. She had stayed at Treeholme only because of Miss Helen, and what she had seen during her years there was enough to make any woman hate any man.

What she had seen? What exactly had she seen? Often she paused to ponder this question. Miss Helen had never wanted for anything; she had always been given everything of the very best—clothes, food, money. Never once had Mrs. Geraint seen Manning strike his daughter; never had she heard his voice raised in anger to her. What was it, then, which had always frightened the child?

Mrs. Geraint could remember times when she had seen

Manning come away from the child's room at night, and she had gone in to find the child rigid with fright. And yet, according to the child, the father had only come in to say "Good night," to caress her with one of those long fingers of his.

No, Manning was certainly not cruel to his child by word or deed; of that Mrs. Geraint was quite certain. But the fact remained that, try as she would, Miss Helen could never hide her fear of her father from her; could never disguise the relief in her face and eyes when he went away for a time; and now and again Mrs. Geraint would catch a glimpse of his face as the father watched the growing child and the grown girl, and the sight of it would come back to disturb her in her sleep at nights.

And once, when she, Mrs. Geraint, had had one of her sleep-walking bouts, she had wakened to find herself gazing into that thin-lipped, narrow, white face with its half-closed eyes and sneering mouth. It had been in the still hours of the dawn, and she had fainted on the spot, recovered to find herself alone, and crawled back to her bed more dead than alive.

Mrs. Geraint took the camera from the butler's hand and gave him, in return, a bit of her mind. Superstitious, indeed! What next? If the camera was broken she would see to it that he paid for it to be repaired; and what business had he picking the pears? Like a great schoolboy, stealing pears like that! Didn't he get enough to eat?

A sound behind them made them both turn. The window of the master's workroom was being opened slowly, and through it, presently, came with the same characteristic slowness, the head of the master himself.

"I think," came in the gentle, rasping voice which always sent a shiver up and down Mrs. Geraint's spine, "that you might choose your place to brawl in a little more cleverly."

There followed a silence while Manning surveyed his two servants through his narrowed eyes, seeming to enjoy the effect upon them of his sudden appearance.

"Mrs. Geraint," he continued presently, "there will be a number of people to dinner here tonight. Miss Helen will be back soon, and she will give you details. You may go."

The portly housekeeper disappeared around the corner of the house, and Manning fixed his gaze upon his butler.

"Come here, Strange," he said presently. The man obeyed, going within a yard of the window. "So you have taken a fancy to the pears outside my workroom window, eh?"

Some new quality in the voice made the man look up, suddenly pale.

"The formula which von Jenn will pay you so handsomely for is not in this room, Gibbon."

The man started violently as he heard himself addressed by this name, and something which might have been a low, rasping chuckle escaped from the thin lips.

"Go about your duties, Strange," continued the voice, "and continue to be the faithful butler. I may yet decide, when I have time to think of it, to communicate with my friends at Scotland Yard. They will be delighted to meet you, believe me. In the meantime, I should do my work here, if I were you, and keep away from this window. It will amuse me to see how faithful you can be, and how cleverly you can keep von Jenn supplied with lies. You may go, Strange."

And Strange went, his breath coming in little gasps, his

face wet with the sweat which was not altogether the result of the oppressive heat.

At Fane Court, fifteen miles away, the two-seater containing Anthony Fane and his friend Teddy Fraser was coming to a snorting stop at the top of the drive. The two occupants slung long legs over the sides and made their way over the lawns to where a number of people sat in low deck-chairs about a tea-table. Doctor Henderson, the local general practitioner, and one of the family in every house for miles around; Helen Manning, lovely, quiet, and with little of the care-free laughter which should be in the eyes of every young girl of twenty; Kay Fane, nineteen, Eton-cropped, too red-lipped, too saucy altogether about the face, and making one think whenever one looked at her how much more piquantly attractive she might have been with the big crop of unruly curls which would have grown on her head if only she would let them; big Bill Brent, solemn, and as wise an owl, as became the private secretary of so important a public man as Sir Anthony Fane; Lady Fane, who spent most of the time saying "Yes, Anthony" to her husband and the rest of it hoping for her son to grow up, and her daughter to grow younger again; and finally Sir Anthony himself, portentous, important, and withal just sufficiently brainless to make even these qualities likeable.

They all looked up as the two young men came towards them over the lawn.

"What's the betting?" Kay wanted to know.

"Rushing at it," growled Sir Anthony. "Serve the boy right if Manning has sent him about his business. Don't know what's coming to this generation. Now in my time…"

"Yes, yes, my dear," said his wife soothingly.

"Queer chap, like Manning, wants careful handling," growled Sir Anthony again, whereat Doctor Henderson tried to make Helen smile by winking at her, and failed dismally, for she smiled only with her lips.

"Oh, cheer up, everybody," said Kay. "What the hell does it matter what the old bird said, anyhow?"

"Kay!" in scandalised tones from her mother. "Your language, my dear! Really! You might consider…"

"Why the deuce don't they elope and have done with it?" went on the girl, taking no notice of the interruption. "All this fuss about a darned engagement! Gruesome, I call it. What's wrong with a swift bunk and a registry office? Helen, my dear, wrap the little swine up and take him off and marry him, for goodness' sake. This fuss is getting on my nerves."

"Suppose we wait and hear what's happened?" Big Bill Brent made his one contribution to the conversation and buried his face in a bun.

"What's the result?" Kay yelled the question at the approaching young men, now some fifty yards away.

"Okay!" came back an answering yell from Mr. Fraser, while his companion tugged at his tie, and his countenance glowed crimson.

Helen sat up in her seat and looked amazed, and a stupefied silence fell upon the whole group until the two arrived, at last, in their midst.

"Won in a canter," announced Mr. Fraser. "Simply walked in on the old boy and bounced him all over the room till he said yes, didn't you, old boy?" He poked the blushing, tie-tugging Anthony in the ribs.

"Well, I don't know that I'd go so far as 'bouncing,'" replied the latter, "but Teddy's quite right in what he says. Your old—your father's given his consent, Helen, and now—er…"

"'… On with the dance, let joy be unconfined,'" murmured Bill Brent.

"Exactly," agreed Mr. Fraser. "Took the very words out of my mouth. But there's more to come. Say on, old cock."

"Well, the fact is," continued Anthony, thus adjured, "the old—I mean Mr. Manning wants us all to go over there to dinner and celebrate the engagement."

A general opening of wide eyes.

"Sent his compliments to the guv'nor and the mater, and threw quite a speech off his chest about the short notice and all that, and I've got to take Helen straight back to cut the bread and butter and lay the jolly old table. Sevenish for cocktails, and whoopee thereafter, and I don't mind telling you, you could all have knocked me down with a feather. Now the question is, what about it? All in favour?"

"Ah—hum"—began Sir Anthony—"sent his compliments, eh?"

"To you and the mater."

"Hm! Yes. I see. No time to come in person, what?"

"Hit the nail right on the head, sir."

"Well, what do you say, Mildred?" Sir Anthony turned to his wife, and got his answer from Kay.

"We're all going. The whole boiling lot of us, and, for Helen's sake, we're going to like it."

"Dash it all, Kay," admonished her brother, "anybody'd think…and after all, it's Helen's house you're talking about."

"Sorry, Helen, old thing," said Kay hastily. "No offence meant, and none took, I hopes?"

Helen Manning jumped up.

"Of course you're all coming," she said, her face a little pale. "Tony darling, you'd better take me back straight away." She went to him and took his arm. "See you all at seven, then?" and then, as they all nodded, "You're to come, Hendy."

For a moment Doctor Henderson hesitated, and then he saw the sudden anxiety in the girl's eyes, and smiled.

"I'll be there, my dear, I'll be there."

Something like relief showed on her face as he answered.

"Then that's all settled. See you at seven."

She turned away, her arm still in that of Anthony's, and the little group at the tea-tables watched them walk across the lawn to the car.

"Poor child!" sighed Lady Fane. "It will be a relief to me when they are married. That child's face…"

Kay sat up in her chair and selected another cigarette.

"Look here, Hendy," she said determinedly, "now we're on the subject, what is the matter with Helen and her father?"

"Kay…!" began Lady Fane in her horrified voice.

"Oh, rabbits!" replied that young lady, blowing a mouthful of smoke into the still air. "Everybody knows something's wrong. It sticks out a mile. What is it, Hendy? You've known them for donkeys' years. Come on, let's have it."

But Doctor Henderson had risen from his chair, and was busy lighting his pipe.

"Nothing's the matter," he said presently. "See you all presently," and bowing to Lady Fane, and waving his hand to the others, he, too, made his way slowly across the lawn, his face, now that the others could not see it, set and grim.

Kay suddenly jumped up from her chair, ran after him, and slipped her hand through his arm.

"I'm sorry, Hendy," she said softly, and her fine eyes, as they looked up at him, bore out the truth of what she said.

"Nothing to be sorry for, Kay, my dear," he replied, his usual smile coming back into his face.

"But it's awful," Kay went on, "to see Helen walking about as if she were in a perpetual state of seeing spooks, and as if she had some secret sorrow, and everybody knows that old Manning is queer…"

Doctor Henderson stopped and placed his hands on the girl's shoulders.

"Look here, Kay, old thing," he said easily, and with a tight little smile on his mouth, "if you're all bothering about Helen and her father, you can take it from me that everything's all right between them. Word of honour," he added, seeing the incredulity in her face.

"Word of honour?" she asked, astonished.

"Word of honour," he replied solemnly. "And now she's going to marry Tony, everything's going to be all right."

He patted her cheek and left her, and for a moment she stood looking after his bowed figure as it walked along.

"The splendid lie!" she said softly to herself. "Good old Hendy!"

Chapter Three

Half-Past Five to Seven

NO RELIEF DURING THIS TIME OF THE OPPRESSIVE HEAT. On the contrary, it seemed to become thicker, heavier, the air more still, and away to the east the sky became filled with a dark blue haze.

For two of the fifteen miles young Anthony Fane sent his two-seater along at its usual exuberant pace when he was driving, and then, seeing the road, which stretched straight ahead of them for another two miles, quite empty, he shut his engine off and brought the car to a stop. Then, turning to the girl at his side, he tugged once or twice at his tie, blushed a vivid scarlet, and spoke.

"I say, Helen."

"Well?"

"I say, we're engaged. I mean to say, it's official."

She smiled at him and, stretching out a dainty hand, she pushed his fingers away from his tortured tie and straightened it.

"If it comes to that," went on the ardent one, "we're

practically married. Just a spot of confetti, and there you are. The trouble is, I can't believe it; can't grasp it, don't you know."

The girl laughed outright—such a rare thing for her, that Anthony looked at her in surprise.

"I shall have to start nagging you," she said.

For answer, he gave his tie another tug and suddenly took her in his arms. Followed a minute's kissing, at the end of which the tie claimed his attention once more, and she watched his fidgeting fingers with amusement.

"But what I wanted to ask you, old thing," he continued, "is why you got so upset when I said I was going to your guv'nor?"

The girl's beautiful face changed as if by magic, the tenderness going out of her eyes, the smile from her lips. She sat back in her seat and stared at the road before them.

"Well, why was it?"

"Well," she answered presently, "it was—was natural, wasn't it?"

He shook his head. "Oh, no, it wasn't just anxiety. You looked scared stiff, as if something awful was going to happen to you. Why was it?"

For a long moment the girl sat, silent and buried in deep thought, and the boy watched her, his face filling with concern as he saw the fear in her eyes. Then suddenly she turned towards him and took his hands.

"Tony, darling," she said, "there's something you ought to know about me…something pretty awful, and I've got to tell you."

"Pretty awful about you? Tripe, darling! There couldn't be anything awful about you."

"But there is, and I've got to tell you. Tony"—she looked up at him for a moment, then bent her head—"I hate my father."

"Hate your father?"

"Yes, I'm afraid of him, and I've been afraid of him all my life, ever since I can remember. It must be wrong to be afraid of one's own father... There must be something terribly wrong with me to—to hate him like I do."

"Good Lord!"

"I've tried all my life to conquer it."

She sat back in her seat again, and the boy gazed at her in astonishment.

"Well," he said presently, "I must say your guv'nor's not everybody's meat. I'm bound to admit that he gives me a turn. Queer way of looking at a bloke, if you know what I mean. But has he ever been cruel to you?"

She shook her head.

"No. He...oh, I can't explain; but ever since I can remember I've—I've been afraid. Whenever he came into a room where I was alone, I—I used to feel as if some torturer was coming to me. At night sometimes he would come... I—I would wake up suddenly and find him looking down on me..." She shuddered violently, and Anthony put his arm about her. "He has never done anything...never struck me, or anything like that, but I'm sure he knows—he has always known—that I hate him and fear him, and he seems to love to watch me when he touches me, or...or makes me kiss him...he seems to gloat." She turned again to him. "Sometimes I think I shall go mad," she went on, "that I can't stick it another day. Oh, Tony, let's be married soon; let's run away tomorrow, tonight—now. Let's just go off by ourselves and never come back. If only I could do that!"

The boy looked at her with troubled face.

"Look here, Helen," he said, "suppose I have a word with the old boy?"

As suddenly as the mood had come to her, it passed. She turned away from her companion and settled herself back in her seat.

"I'm sorry, Tony, darling," she said in a hard little voice. "You mustn't take any notice of me. I'm just nervy, and of course everything's going to be all right. It is, isn't it?"

"Of course it is, sweetheart. We're going to be married straight away."

"And he did say yes, didn't he?"

"He said it was excellent, and shook hands, and here we all are coming over to dinner. It's all okay. Of course it's okay!"

"Just forget what I said then, darling. It doesn't matter now. It won't be long before I…I shall leave that house."

Followed another minute of kisses, and it might have been two, or even three and more, had not young Mr. Fane suddenly been made aware by the impatient blare of a hooter behind him, that his car was blocking the road. With a scarlet face he pressed the starter and drew his car to one side to allow a big limousine to pass. The smile on the face of the chauffeur merely deepened the crimson on Anthony's face, and just by way of giving vent to his feelings, he sent the two-seater after the other car and sailed past it with his nose well in the air.

At the door of Treeholme Helen dismissed her fiancé, firmly refusing to allow him even to leave his car and come to the door with her, much less into the house itself. There was much for her to do, and little time in which to do it. She knew, too, that she must see her father, and she was anxious to get the interview over and done with.

She found him in his study. He was seated behind his table, poring again over the album of photographs, his thin face cupped in his hands, and he did not alter his position as she came through the doorway and paused on the threshold.

"Ah! Here you are at last."

"Here I am, Father." She advanced nervously into the room and stopped, uncertainly, half-way to the table. He made an imperceptible gesture with his head towards the chair opposite him—the chair in which Anthony had sat not long before.

"Sit down, Helen."

She obeyed him, seating herself upon the edge of the chair.

"Well?"

She looked up, met his half-closed eyes, and looked away again.

"Anthony has told me, Father," she said in reply. "I…I am terribly glad you found yourself able to…to give your consent."

He said nothing for a few moments; merely watched her as she sat there. When he spoke, his voice was lower, more purring than usual.

"You love this young man, Helen?"

"Yes, Father."

"Excellent! Excellent!"

She looked up at him with a little start.

"A good thing to start married life with, my child. Love… love. It means so much, does it not? It fills one's entire mind, and life, and thoughts. Yes, an excellent thing, love; excellent! It so colours the world about us, so mercifully and deceitfully blinds us to the realities of things and people."

Helen looked up astonished. For once his eyes were not upon her; they seemed fixed upon the album which lay open before him on the table. He continued to speak as if to himself.

"So very near to hatred, too, is it not? Merely degrees of the same thing—love and hatred, and how very easily the one develops into the other!"

He rose suddenly to his feet, and Helen did likewise.

"Why do you speak to me like this, Father? What… what…" She paused, her breast rising and falling rapidly as her breathing quickened.

"Yes?"

Helen tried to smile and failed miserably.

"Nothing at all—nothing. Hadn't I better go and see Mrs. Geraint about the dinner?"

"And that is all you have to say to me on an occasion like this, Helen?"

"Why, I—I—there doesn't seem anything else to say."

He turned away from her and walked to the French windows at the far end of the room. Helen watched him as he stood against them, his back turned towards her, his head bowed in thought, and suddenly something stirred deep down in her. He—this man—was, after all, her father; the only relative, as far as she knew, that she had. His blood flowed in her veins, she belonged to him. Perhaps the something that stirred her at that moment was a longing for sympathy, for companionship—not of a friend, not even of a lover—but of somebody who was of her own blood. Perhaps, if she made one effort now, whatever it was which had made her so afraid of him could be swept away. Perhaps she could move him to some act of tenderness, make him understand how lonely she had been all her life. There was no reason, after all, for her fear and dread of him. She was his daughter; he was her father.

She made a step towards him.

"Father…"

He wheeled round suddenly at the sound of her voice. The smile had disappeared from his mouth, leaving it a thin, straight line; the eyes had narrowed until they were mere slits.

Helen recoiled the step she had taken towards him, but the next second his face had changed again, and now wore its accustomed little smile.

"Well, Helen?" He came slowly back to the table and stood looking down on the open album. He raised his head, studied his daughter carefully for a moment, and then looked down again at the album. Helen steadied herself and went on speaking.

"Father, I… Surely this is a time when we two should… should try to understand each other…" She trailed off into silence, and he transferred his gaze from the album to her again.

"Yes? Go on."

"We never seem to…to have been—how can I put it?— very near to each other, have we? I mean I…I don't quite know how to put it… You have never even told me about…about my mother, I have never even seen a picture of her. Why?"

Manning continued to stand in silence, looking down on the album, his finger gently smoothing his cheek.

Presently, and as if he had suddenly made up his mind about something, he looked up at her and said in his quiet, purring voice:

"Here is your mother, Helen. Come and look at her."

Helen joined him at the table and bent eagerly over the

open page, gazing wonderingly at the portrait which was pasted there.

It was a large photograph of a young girl, perhaps a year or two older than Helen herself, dressed in the summer fashion of twenty-five years ago. She was seated, her body leaning forwards towards the camera, and one hand outstretched to grasp the collar of a big retriever dog which stood at her side, and which strained forward, its teeth showing in a snarl. Her face was raised and her large, wide-opened eyes stared straight into the camera.

Helen gazed long and silently at the portrait. The snarling dog, the fear and appeal in the face of the girl fascinated her.

"That is your mother, Helen. You are very like her."

Helen studied the portrait with a new interest. Yes, now she came to look at it from this angle, she was like the portrait; so very like it, in fact, that it might have been—the difference in the style of dress and coiffure apart—a portrait of herself.

"She looks…" Helen turned to her father who was watching her intently.

"Yes?"

"Afraid. What was it she was afraid of? The dog, too…"

Manning continued to contemplate her in silence, and as she faced him a sudden courage came to her.

"Why have you never told me about my mother?" she demanded. "Until now I had never even seen a picture of her, and all these years you had this here." She pointed to the album on the table at her side. "What does it all mean, Father? I have a right to know."

For answer Manning turned away from her and went to the window again, and as she watched him standing there, the sudden wave of courage left her, and the old fear of him took its place.

"You shall know in good time, Helen," he said to her presently over his shoulder. "All in good time, my girl; and in the meantime you had better go and confer with Mrs. Geraint, and prepare for tonight's joyous occasion."

The words "joyous occasion" came with a curious emphasis which might have been a sneer. Helen stared at him for a moment, then turned to the door. She would never understand this man who was her father, never fathom the dread with which he always filled her.

He spoke again as she reached the door.

"You have not told me, Helen," he said, "when you are to be married. I suppose you have settled the date?"

"No…no…we haven't settled anything yet."

"Hm!" Manning came back to the table, and looked down at the portrait. "You will wish it to be soon, no doubt?"

"Yes… I suppose so… I don't know…"

"Yes, no doubt, you will wish it to be soon. Love is impatient, eh? It was in my young days. And you love this young man, eh?"

"Yes, of course, Father… I told you…"

"Excellent! Excellent!" Manning had not taken his eyes off the portrait while he had spoken to her, and he still remained gazing down at it. He joined his hands together, rubbing them gently against each other, and the little smile broadened on his lips. "Excellent!" he repeated a third time. "Yes, you shall know about your mother all in good time. As you pointed out, you have a right to know."

Helen opened the door and passed through it. Just before

she closed it behind her, she heard him say again "Excellent! Excellent!" as if he was gloating over something.

Once outside the room some of the fear left her, as it always did when she left his presence, and she ran lightly up the stairs to her own room and closed the door behind her.

So that was her mother? That girl with the frightened eyes, the suffering face? The dog, too…

There must be some mystery in it all. She would get hold of old Hendy and ask him if he knew anything about it. He had known her father. Perhaps he would tell her something… perhaps he had even known her mother…

Chapter Four

Half-Past Five to Seven (Continued)

BACK AT FANE COURT, WHAT WAS LEFT OF THE TEA-party continued to sit beneath the trees after Doctor Henderson had left.

Kay came back from her brief conversation with him, and flopped into a chair.

"Hendy," she remarked, selecting another cigarette, "is a rotten liar."

"Kay, my dear…" began Lady Fane in her querulous little voice, and Sir Anthony, receiving his usual cue, promptly interrupted her with a noisy clearance of his throat.

"Lot of nonsense," he boomed. "What should be wrong between Manning and the girl? Just because she walks about looking a bit serious! Lots of people do. Can't all go about grinning like Cheshire cats. Nonsense!" And having settled the matter satisfactorily to himself, Sir Anthony bit the end off a cigar and lit it.

"Nonsense?" Kay sat up in her chair, the light of battle in her eye. "Don't talk through your hat, Pop…"

"Kay, my dear…"

"Look at old Manning," continued Kay, ignoring, as usual, her mother's feeble protest. "D'you mean to tell me he doesn't look funny?"

"Funny? What d'you mean—funny?" Sir Anthony snorted and glared across at his daughter, who returned the glare with interest.

"Funny," she replied with spirit. "Unusual, if you like, abnormal, horrible. Fancy living with him! Fancy trying to eat your eggs and bacon every morning with that sneering, horrible face looking at you across the table. Ugh!" Here Miss Fane indulged in a violent shudder, and brushed some ash off her skirt.

"Manning," Sir Anthony continued the debate, "is a man of—ah—distinction: a scientist with an international reputation, and I've heard it said in more than one quarter that he's in the running for a title of some sort. Reward for important work he's been doing for the government. Man can't be funny if he gets a title."

Kay exploded noisily and brought another "Kay, my dear…" from her long-suffering mother.

"I like that," she said, when she had mastered the emotion aroused by her father's last pronouncement. "Oh, I love that! Why, it's well known that there are more screws loose in the House of Lords than in any other collection of men in the country. And, what is more," she declared, struggling out of her low chair, "I'm going to get at the bottom of the Manning mystery. If old Hendy won't tell me, then I'll find out myself if I have to go and tackle the old bird himself. I'll do it tonight."

"You'll do what tonight?"

Kay approached her father's chair and made a face at him.

"I'll jolly well ask him where he got his face from, why he looks like he does, why Helen always looks so scared, why he never sent her to a decent school, and what he meant by keeping her cooped up in that old barn of a house all her life. Why, if Tony hadn't come across her, if we hadn't asked her here a bit, she'd never have met anybody. I'll ask..."

"You'll ask him nothing of the sort, my girl. The idea!"

Sir Anthony puffed out his cheeks. "Can't go to a man's house and insult him," he continued.

The light of mischief gleamed in Kay's eyes.

"Can't I?" She flicked the ash of her cigarette, letting it fall upon her father's bald head. "Can't I? Oho! We'll see. Just you wait. Just you wait, my lad!"

And Kay danced off towards the house, followed by a "Kay, my dear..." from her mother, and a quiet smile from Bill Brent.

Teddy Fraser got up and followed her with a view to placing before her, for the fourth time that day, the suggestion that he and she should enter together the state of holy matrimony, and the three who were thus left under the trees, fell into silence. Bill Brent lit his pipe and abandoned himself to thought; Sir Anthony devoted himself to his cigar, and Lady Fane picked up the book she had been trying to read earlier on in the afternoon, and held it upside down before her.

It was Lady Fane who broke the silence at last.

"Of course," she said, "Mr. Manning is unpopular in the district, and people do talk..."

"Talk? What people?" The question came gruffly from her husband.

"Oh, I don't know. One hears things. He is rather a strange man, after all, isn't he?"

"Stuff and nonsense! Just because a man doesn't mix much with the rest of the county, and—ah—looks a little odd…"

"He certainly looks odd…"

"Not his fault. Dammit, the man's a genius! Recognised as such, and you can't expect geniuses to look like other people. They don't. Always are a bit queer. Nothing to do with us, anyhow, and Helen's all right. We needn't see anything of him once they're married, and what the deuce he wanted to ask us over there for tonight, I don't know."

"It will be the first time any entertainment has taken place at Treeholme since—well, I don't remember hearing of any before."

"Except when he's been away, and Helen has had us over there for tennis." This was Bill Brent's first contribution to the conversation. He tapped out his pipe and put it away in his pocket. "I think I'll be getting ready," he said, rising. "I said I would go and have a cocktail with Henderson, and I can go over to Treeholme with him."

Sir Anthony nodded absently, and Brent walked slowly away in the direction of the house.

Half an hour later he was driving his own little Austin Seven out through the gates of Fane Court, and it was just after six when he arrived at the doctor's house which stood in the middle of the one street of Maylings, the little village which stood some three miles away from Fane Court, on the road to Treeholme.

He found Doctor Henderson already dressed, and in the act of mixing himself a drink.

"Ah, Bill! I wondered if you would remember the earlier appointment," Henderson greeted him. "Whisky or a mixture? Help yourself."

"Too hot for a cocktail," replied Brent. "I'll make it a long one." He took the whisky bottle and mixed himself a drink. "It's getting hotter, too, unless I'm mistaken."

"Thunder about," observed the doctor, settling himself down in a chair, "and between you and myself, Brent, I wish to goodness I hadn't to wear a boiled shirt on a night like this. Why the devil they can't reform men's dress is beyond me. Well!" He raised his glass and nodded. Brent nodded in return and sipped his drink.

"It's a worthy occasion, anyhow," he remarked with his usual gruffness. "Glad to see Helen happy."

"Yes…yes…poor child!"

Brent looked up suddenly at the other's remark, and glanced keenly at the old doctor. Henderson had lapsed into thought, and his face wore a far-away wistful look.

Brent studied him for a moment before he spoke again.

"Why d'you say that, Henderson?"

"Say what? Eh?"

"Poor child! You were talking about Helen. I just wondered what made you say that."

Henderson looked down into his drink. "Oh, I don't know," he replied thoughtfully. "Not much of a life for a girl like her at Treeholme, is it?"

"So they were saying up at the house before I came away."

"Hm! Yes, I dare say, I dare say."

Henderson toyed again with his glass, and presently sighed heavily.

"Well," he said, rising to his feet, "perhaps it will all come right, now. Let's hope so, anyhow."

"Perhaps?"

Henderson swallowed the rest of his drink and laughed shortly.

"Phew! This heat!" He walked to the window and looked out at his small garden. "We'd better be getting along, eh? Have another drink?"

Brent finished his drink and put his glass down.

"Not for me, thanks," he replied, and then, as he, too, rose from his chair: "What's the matter with Manning?"

"Matter with him?"

"He must be a queer sort of fellow, from all I've heard. Lady Fane was saying after you left that there'd been a good deal of talk in the district. What's it all about?"

Henderson paused before replying. "Must be because he's a bit of a hermit," he said presently. "You know what people are." He turned from the window and faced the other. "Manning's a research chemist," he went on, "and ever since I've known him, he's devoted his life to it. No time for anything else, in fact; sort of shut himself away from the world more and more every year, and—well, I suppose that sort of thing is bound to have its effect sooner or later. He is a queer fellow, there's no doubt about that; eccentric, and so on; they all are, these research geniuses."

"I see." Brent nodded thoughtfully at the other's explanation. "'Much learning hath made him mad,' eh?"

"Mad?" Henderson turned suddenly and stared at Brent. "Mad, did you say? Who said he was mad?"

"Nobody—nobody at all."

"He's not mad. For God's sake, Brent, don't start that rumour again…"

"Why, was it ever started before, then?"

Henderson shuffled his feet. "No, I mean, don't mention the word, if only for Helen's sake," he went on hastily. "She's pitied enough already because of his—his eccentricity. Don't add insanity to it…"

"But, good Lord, Henderson! I wasn't suggesting…"

"No, of course not." Henderson smiled with an effort, and mopped his brow with his handkerchief. "This heat!" he said. "It's getting worse."

"But, look here, Henderson, old man, I wasn't suggesting that Manning's insane. Why, I…"

Henderson patted Brent's shoulder.

"No, of course not," he said with another attempt at a smile. "I was merely thinking of Helen, and—and—the general idiocy and credulity of people. She's got enough to put up with already, goodness knows."

Brent would have liked to know what exactly it was that Helen Manning had to put up with, but he felt, suddenly, that he was on dangerous ground.

"Better be getting along, eh?" he said, picking up his hat.

Henderson led the way to the door, and Brent followed him through it, and presently the two friends were fitting themselves into Brent's small car.

Not the slightest breeze stirred the still, close air. Away to the east the dark blue haze was creeping slowly nearer across the sky.

Chapter Five

Seven to Quarter-Past Eight

KAY, TEDDY FRASER, AND ANTHONY WERE THE FIRST TO arrive at Treeholme, the fifteen miles and one bewildered and ill-fated hen having been covered by the latter's car at an average speed of what the critical owner described as a "quiet forty."

Kay swung two shapely, silk-clad legs over the side, heaved the rest of herself after them, and surveyed the house while she finished her cigarette.

"The ogre's castle," she remarked, dropping the ash from her cigarette into the hat which Mr. Fraser was holding in his hand. "The lair of the dragon. The…"

"Come on," said her brother, passing her and mounting the steps to the big porch. "And remember this," he continued as he pressed the bell-button, "you've jolly well got to play up tonight, Kay. Cut out the funny stuff. The old boy's no ordinary bird, and if you start anything…"

The opening of the door cut short his remarks, and as he stepped to one side to allow his sister to enter the house, that young lady favoured him with a violent and remarkable contortion of her features before sailing past the waiting Strange into the house.

"Miss Fane, *Master* Fane, and Mr. Edward Fraser," she proclaimed to the surrounding air in a loud voice, and as Strange bowed in acknowledgment of her announcement, a door on their left opened quietly, and Kay saw Horace Manning for the second time in her life.

He had pushed the door wide open behind him, and stood in the doorway surveying her through his half-closed eyes. Kay stared back at him, taking in every detail of the tall, thin, immaculately clad figure, and it was she who broke the tension which somehow crept into the situation by presently advancing towards him with outstretched hand.

"Ah, Mr. Manning!" she exclaimed brightly.

Manning took her hand and looked down on her.

"You are Miss Fane?"

"I am, and although I've seen you before, this is the first time we've met. Isn't that a great thought?"

He dropped her hand, and his eyebrows went up slightly over the narrowed eyes. Anthony, who, with Mr. Fraser, was awaiting his cue, gasped at Kay's next remark.

"I've heard such a lot about you, Mr. Manning."

"Really?"

"Yes. Are you looking pleased at the moment or pained? Yours, you know, is the sort of face which would look the same in either case. So clever of you, I think."

Anthony gasped again and stepped forward, plucking nervously at his tie.

"You mustn't take any notice of my sister, sir," he explained. "She's only a nitwit really. This is her idea of being bright."

Manning transferred his disconcerting gaze from Kay to Anthony and, as usual, paused before replying.

"I think your sister is charming," he purred.

"There you are!" said Kay briskly, and then, to Manning: "And I don't think you are half so awful as people say you are, dear Mr. Manning."

Anthony groaned aloud.

Manning performed his favourite trick of rubbing his cheek gently with one finger.

"I'm delighted to hear it," he said gently, "delighted. That, however, would still leave room for quite a lot of—er—awfulness though, I take it?"

"Quite a lot," agreed Kay. "And now, having got this over, and you and I having fallen in love with each other at first sight, Mr. Manning, where's Helen? Not down yet?"

Helen herself appeared at that moment, running down the stairs.

"Here is the heroine of the occasion," said Manning, waving one long-fingered hand in the direction of the stairs, and at the sound of her father's voice Helen flushed painfully and tried to hide it by kissing Kay. She looked tired, and about her eyes lurked a suspicion of recent weeping.

"Bring your wrap upstairs, Kay dear," she said, and with a nod to Anthony and Teddy, she led the way to the stairs. Kay followed her, and Anthony, now in a state of misery at what he regarded as his sister's unfortunate opening of the evening, surrendered his hat to the waiting Strange.

Mr. Fraser did likewise, and Manning stepped on one side to allow them to enter the room behind.

"Er—great idea of yours, sir," commenced Anthony nervously.

"A great idea?"

"This dinner. What d'you say, young Fraser?"

That young gentleman, thus appealed to, cleared his throat and smiled jovially.

"Magnificent," he agreed. "Jolly sporting, I call it." He coughed, blushed, and shifted from one foot to the other.

"Er—congratulate you, sir," he mumbled.

"Congratulate me? On what?"

Teddy stared.

"On the engagement, sir. Your daughter's engagement."

"Ah! To be sure!" Manning's curious little smile broadened imperceptibly. "We mustn't forget the engagement, must we?"

The two men looked at each other, both at a loss. Teddy tried to step into the breach.

"Mr. Manning pulling your leg, young Fane," he remarked breezily, and then winked solemnly at Manning, who received the gesture without sign. "These young lovers, sir, eh? 'Love that makes the world go round,' what? Ah, well, we were all young once." Teddy settled himself back in the chair and gazed dreamily at the ceiling. "Why, sir," he continued, "I dare say you yourself once got Cupid's dart right in the bull's eye, eh? I mean, I shouldn't wonder."

He inclined his head towards his host with a view to the bestowal of another wink, and as his eye met the older man's face, he sat up suddenly; for he had caught that face in a momentary convulsion of rage and hatred which made him catch at his breath. A second later and he would have missed the spasm which had come and gone in a flash. He glanced at Anthony, but that young man was fingering his tie, his crimson face turned towards the floor at his feet. Anthony apparently had seen nothing.

Teddy turned again to Manning, to find him on his feet.

"I'm sorry, sir," he began, "if I—er—spoke out of my turn. Most frightfully sorry. No intention to offend, sir."

"Why, what's all this?" Anthony was on his feet, staring at the other two. Then Teddy rose, slowly, and uncomfortably, and for a moment of silence the three stood and stared at each other.

"I'm—er—sorry, sir," repeated Teddy, and immediately Manning held up his hand.

"There is nothing whatever for you to reproach yourself with, Mr.—er—Fraser; nothing at all."

"Oh, I'm—er—jolly glad to hear it; jolly glad, sir."

For another moment Manning contemplated the two embarrassed young men through his half-closed eyes, then he walked slowly to the door, turning back to them as he reached it.

"You will excuse me?" he asked. "A small matter in my laboratory which demands my attention." And without waiting for a reply, he opened the door. "Strange will bring you some—er—cocktails, and I have no doubt the young ladies will be down soon." Another glance from his queer eyes, and he had closed the door softly behind him.

"Well!" Teddy sank down into his seat. "Of all the…!"

"What was it all about? What the dickens were you talking about? What upset him?" Anthony came and stood over his friend. "One moment everything seemed all right, and the next…"

Teddy waved a hand.

"Don't ask me," he said. "He's off his rocker; bats; that's what's the matter with him. My sainted aunt!" And he passed a hand over a perspiring brow.

"But what happened? Come on, cough it up, young Fraser. What did you get up to?"

"I? I didn't get up to anything. I just said something about us both being young once—you know, just tried a spot of light badinage on the old geyser, and—Phoo! did you see his face?"

"What happened to his face?"

"Murder, my lad. Pure, unadulterated murder in the first degree."

"What do you mean?"

"I mean that he looked murder." Teddy shuddered, in spite of the heat. "If ever a man looked murder, he did then. I just happened to look up at the moment, and—I tell you honestly, young Fane, old Manning's off his rocker. He's as mad as... Good God! no wonder Helen looks like she does, living with somebody like that."

Anthony was about to reply when the door opened and Doctor Henderson and Bill Brent entered. They were followed by Strange carrying a tray laden with shaker and glasses, which he put down and left, and as the door closed behind him Brent turned to Anthony.

"What's the matter with you two?" he wanted to know.

"I was telling Tony..." began Teddy, when Anthony cut him short.

"He's been talking through his hat," he explained. "Some rot about old Manning giving him a look, or something of the sort..."

"And so he did, by Jove!" Teddy interrupted him. "We

were talking about young love, chipping Tony here about the engagement, and I said something to Manning about us all being young once, and suffering from it, and I happened to look up at him and caught him looking at me as if he wanted to murder me. In my opinion…"

"Where's Helen?" demanded the doctor, interrupting Teddy.

"Upstairs with Kay," replied Anthony.

"No, here we are." Kay, followed by Helen, sailed into the room, and stopped short at the sight of the four men's faces. "Nice, gay-looking lot you are, too!" she remarked. "This is going to be some party. Here's Helen, who says she's got a head fit to burst…"

"I didn't," Helen interrupted her, and was promptly shouted down by the other.

"Well, you look as if you had, anyway; and here you all are, looking as if you'd heard of a murder or something. Where's Mr. Manning?"

"Said he had to go to his laboratory," Teddy replied.

"Then I'll go and dig him out," Kay declared, turning to the door. "Where is the laboratory?"

"Look here, Kay," began Anthony, "you've done enough for one evening. You jolly well stay here."

"Rabbits!" returned Kay. "Besides, I'd like to see what his laboratory's like, anyhow. If nobody'll tell me where it is"—she looked round at the others—"I shall have to find it for myself."

She might have carried out her threat, but the door opened, and Strange announced Sir Anthony and Lady Fane.

"Well, here we are at last," boomed Sir Anthony, and looked

around for his host. "Manning not here?" he demanded as he accepted a cocktail from Bill Brent.

"I'm going to find him," declared Kay. She made for the door, pulled it open, and stepped back with a half-smothered little cry; for Manning stood in the doorway, and continued to stand there quite still, only his eyes moving under the half-closed lids as they took in each member of the group in the room.

Presently he advanced slowly into the room and singled out Lady Fane, bowing over her hand with old-fashioned courtesy.

"You will pardon my remissness in not being here to welcome you when you came," he said in his purring voice. "And you, too, Sir Anthony"—turning to the baronet. "An experiment of some importance which I am conducting in my laboratory," he continued as he turned to the only member of the visitors whom he did not know as yet—Brent, "demanded my attention."

"How exciting!" exclaimed Kay. "Mr. Manning," she continued, slipping her arm through his, "I'm going to get you to show me that laboratory after dinner. Do you have explosions and things?"

"Kay, my dear…" from Lady Fane, and Manning turned and looked down at the girl at his side.

"I will be very happy to show you what I am doing." He turned to the others. "But we are here to celebrate an engagement,—are we not?—and not to discuss anything so dull as chemistry."

"Is it so very dull, then?"

"You shall see for yourself after dinner, Miss Fane."

Kay was about to make a reply to this when Strange appeared and announced dinner. Manning disengaged his arm from Kay's and offered it to Lady Fane with one of his courtly little bows.

In silence Helen marshalled the remainder of her guests, and they made their way across the hall to the dining-room.

It was as they were about to seat themselves that the first distant rumble of thunder made itself heard.

"Going to be a storm," boomed Sir Anthony, from his position on Helen's right at the bottom of the table.

Manning looked up quickly and scanned his guests.

"Yes," he remarked. "There is going to be a storm."

Chapter Six

Quarter-Past Eight to Ten

"THEN WE REALLY OUGHT..." BEGAN LADY FANE, AND pulled herself up short, and Kay laughed outright.

"Not going, Mother? You can't be going to suggest that we really ought to be going before we start dinner? How priceless!"

Lady Fane cast a shocked look in her daughter's direction. "Kay, my dear..." she said, horrified. "I was not going to suggest any such thing. What would you have Mr. Manning think of us?"

"From the way he looks at us, I should say that he thinks we are a collection of things in jars."

There was a general gasp at Kay's audacity, a short laugh from Teddy Fraser, and a muttered "There she goes again" from Anthony, ending in a groan. Manning was the only one at the table who did not seem put out, and he smiled at Kay as she continued:

"You know, Mr. Manning, you really have a way of looking at one as if one was something on the end of a pin. Do we really look like that, or are you just making a reputation?"

"Rising generation," growled Sir Anthony from the end of the table. "Mustn't take any notice of 'em, Manning, eh?" He tried to manage a laugh and narrowly avoided a choking fit, and it was Manning himself who diverted attention from the worthy baronet to himself.

"Well," he remarked, "I suppose, really, that we are all on pins."

"On pins?" Lady Fane shot a warning glance at her daughter whose eyes were lighting up. "How very interesting! And how uncomfortable! On pins!"

"I was about to say," continued Manning in his smooth voice, "on the pins of our own emotions. What are ambition, fear, hatred, suffering"—he seemed to roll the word around his tongue—"but pins at the end of which we struggle more or less inefficiently through our lives. A man's ambition, for instance, will stick itself into him, raise him out of normality, and dangle him about feebly in the air until, at last, it drops him either into the gutter of failure, or into the mud of disillusionment."

He paused and looked round the table. Henderson was staring down into his soup, seemingly lost in thought. Brent, who sat next to him, was staring straight at the speaker, a little frown of thought between his eyes. Kay, too, was looking at him, the light of mischief in her eyes. Teddy and Anthony, the latter fiddling with his tie with one hand, stared stonily before them, as did also Sir Anthony.

Manning found his daughter's eyes fixed upon him, and to her he seemed to address the remainder of his words.

"Fear," he went on. "Think of the wrigglings of the afraid." He laughed. "Those who live in fear never have their feet on the ground. Hatred too. Imagine how hatred can dominate a life, a brain; how it can eat its way into thoughts until they become diseased. What is a man who hates but something on the end of a pin? And, until his hatred is satisfied, how can he hope to escape from it?"

Helen gave an involuntary little gasp, and as one, the other heads turned in her direction. She sat quite still, white to the lips, her eyes fixed upon those of her father as if under the influence of some deadly fascination. Anthony, who sat next to her, stretched out one hand beneath the table, found hers and pressed it; and at the feel of her lover's hand her tenseness relaxed suddenly, and the colour rushed back into her face. She dropped her eyes to the table before her, and the others, greatly wondering, took their gaze off her, and transferred it back to their host as he continued his explanation:

"Suffering, again," he went on, "suffering; the agony of tortured nerves, the slow yielding of the mind to mental anguish; the futile wrigglings of the tortured…"

His nostrils distended as he inhaled a deep breath, and the eyes all but closed.

"Now look at him," whispered Teddy to Anthony at his side. "Just look at the blighter!"

Anthony looked and drew his breath in with a little hiss. His right hand still held Helen's beneath the table, and he turned quickly as he felt her move. She was half out of her chair, her other hand raised to her head.

"I… I…" she said, and would have fallen had not Anthony risen and put his arm about her.

In a trice Henderson was out of his seat and at her side, and there was a general clatter of silver against china as spoons were laid in plates.

The doctor pressed Helen back into her chair and raised her wine to her lips. She tried to push his hand away, but he insisted, and she sipped it slowly.

"It's the thunder in the air, I expect," he said. "Come and lie down for a few minutes. I'm sure everybody will excuse you. Come, Helen."

Kay got to her feet.

"I'll come with you, Helen, darling," she said, and was about to move around the table when Manning spoke again.

"Please don't disturb yourselves. If Helen will come with me to the laboratory, I feel sure…" He left the sentence unfinished, and Henderson felt a shudder pass through the girl's frame.

"No…no…" she whispered. "It is nothing at all. Just a little dizziness. It's the thunder, I expect. I'm terribly sorry… Please, everybody… Hendy…"

"But, darling, you look like nothing on earth." Anthony, the anxious lover, bent across the table to her. "Are you sure, Helen…?"

Helen pulled herself together with a little jerk and drank some more wine.

"There," she said, her lips forming themselves into a smile, "it's passed. It was nothing at all. Don't let's spoil our engagement dinner, Tony." She took his hand in the sight of everybody, and gave it a little squeeze and put it away from her.

The night outside filled again with the rumble of thunder, still distant, but nearer this time, and somebody started a discussion upon storms. It was a discussion in which Manning took no part, unless appealed to, when he answered with a monosyllable or a smile. Brent, who watched him throughout, noticed that his eyes went continually to his daughter who had suddenly become almost feverishly gay.

Presently champagne was brought and served, and Manning pushed his chair back and rose to his feet, glass in hand.

"We must drink to the happiness of our young lovers," he said, "otherwise the occasion would not be complete. What is more beautiful than the spectacle of the first blissful love? Such a picture of happiness, faith, hope, such a contrast to disillusionment, is it not? It is a wonderful thing to drink to, my friends—as wonderful as a dream."

He raised his glass.

"My dear daughter," he said, and Brent remarked the faintest curling of the lip, "I drink to your happiness."

But before he could do so, Helen was on her feet, two spots of feverish colour in her cheeks, her eyes shining with unnatural brightness. She concentrated her gaze upon her father, and the two faced each other across the table.

"Father," she said, and Brent thought he detected a note of defiance in her voice, "I am going to be happy. Nothing shall ever take it away from me. I am going to be happy."

Anthony stood by her side and slipped an arm around her.

"You leave that to me, darling," he said, and together they stood and looked across the table at Manning, who stood with his long fingers playing nervously with the stem of his glass.

Again Manning's glass was raised towards his lips, but it never reached them, for suddenly the slender stem snapped, and the bowl of the glass crashed on to the plate on the table beneath him. He opened his hand. The broken stem followed the bowl to the plate, and he stood quietly watching a thin stream of blood trickle downwards from his fingers and over the palm of his hand. Two crimson stains appeared suddenly on the whiteness of the table-cloth, and Manning raised his head. For once his lips were drawn back over his teeth in a smile.

"If you will excuse me," he said, backing behind his chair, and he turned and left the room in the complete silence which had fallen upon them all.

Henderson mopped his brow with his handkerchief and looked across at Helen and Anthony. Her eyes were still fixed on the door through which her father had disappeared, and with his going the feverish colour had drained from her face, leaving it pale again. Suddenly she seemed to relax, and would have fallen back into her seat, had not Anthony's arm been there to hold her up.

The doctor rose quickly to his feet and raised his glass.

"We haven't drunk the toast," he said breezily. "Helen, my dear, and you, Anthony, here's our love to you, and all happiness."

The others rose and raised their glasses in obedience to the doctor's lead. Kay and her mother hurried to Helen's side and kissed her, while Teddy seized Anthony's hand and pumped it vigorously up and down. Henderson took advantage of the general concentration on Helen and Anthony to slip from the room in search of Manning.

He found the scientist seated in his study before the open album on his table. He had wrapped a handkerchief about his cut hand, and looked up as the doctor entered.

"Ah, Henderson!" he said.

The doctor went to the table and looked down at the photographs in the album.

"I thought I might be of use, Manning," he said. "Is your hand cut very badly?"

"A mere nothing, my dear Henderson; a mere nothing. I used it as an excuse to get away to my laboratory. In a few minutes now I am to know the result of my experiment. Perhaps you will be good enough to help Helen look after my guests until I return."

Doctor Henderson stood stroking his chin with one hand for a moment before he looked up and met the other's eyes.

"Very well, then," he said at last, and walked slowly to the door, at which he paused again, as if turning something over in his mind. Once again he looked up and caught the other's eyes upon him. There was a gleam of quiet mockery in them, and without uttering a word, Henderson opened the door and passed through it.

Chapter Seven

Ten to Eleven

DOCTOR HENDERSON WAS HALF-WAY ACROSS THE HALL on his way back to the dining-room, when the sound of a door slamming behind him made him stop and turn.

A maid was hurrying towards him, her face filled with excitement and anxiety.

"Doctor Henderson," she said in an agitated voice as she came up to him, "it's Mrs. Geraint. She's took ill in the kitchen."

"Taken ill?"

"Yes, sir. It's the cat and the kittens, sir, and will you come straight away. We don't know what to do with her."

The doctor opened his mouth to ask what on earth the cat and the kittens had to do with Mrs. Geraint's being ill, thought better of it, and followed the girl through a door at the back of the hall, and down the corridor which led to the big kitchen.

The portly housekeeper was stretched out on the floor. One distracted maid was busily slapping her hands, while another held a bottle of smelling-salts beneath the prostrate one's nose. The Doctor motioned them to one side and bent over the patient.

It proved to be nothing more serious than a deep faint, and in less than a minute he had her seated on a chair, while he slowly coaxed her back to consciousness.

"He's taken the cat and her kittens," she murmured feebly when she had managed to open her eyes.

"What does she mean by that?" Henderson asked the maids who stood looking on.

"It's the master, sir," one of them replied. "He's taken the cat and her kittens into the lab., sir, for his experiments. Mrs. Geraint's been carrying on about it all the evening, sir, working herself up something awful, sir, and it was as much as we could do to stop her going and making a scene in the dining-room, sir."

"But she wouldn't faint because of that, surely?"

"No, sir. It must be the heat, sir. Mrs. Geraint never could abide thunder, neither, could she, Alice?"

The other maid nodded her head in agreement. "She was that fond of the cat, sir, and I dessay she got all upset on her account, what with the kittens too. She's been swearing she'll go straight to the cruelty people in the morning, and carrying on alarming, she has. I think she ought to go to bed."

Henderson nodded his head.

"Very wise, too. D'you hear that, Mrs. Geraint?" he said to the seated woman, raising his voice.

She sighed heavily and opened her eyes again.

"You'd better get up to bed, d'you hear, and have a strong cup of tea. Do you more good than brandy. Get a good sleep, eh?"

Mrs. Geraint sat up in the chair.

"Wouldn't have had this happen on Miss Helen's engagement day for anything," she said weakly, beginning to cry. "He took my cat, he did…and the kittens… Pretty little things they are…"

"Yes, yes; never mind about that. You leave it to me, Mrs. Geraint, and get yourself up to bed. You need a good night's sleep."

"I've been feeling that queer all the evening, sir. It's the thunder about. It always does upset me."

Henderson straightened himself and looked down on her.

"No doubt about it," he said soothingly. "A night in bed, and you'll be as right as a trivet in the morning. Come now, Mrs. Geraint, up with you."

He helped her to her feet, and then handed her over to the care of the two maids.

"You'll speak to the master about my cat, sir?" she asked as he turned to go.

"I'll speak to him, never fear."

"I'm fond of the animal, sir, and I can't bear to think of those little kittens being tortured, sir."

"Nonsense! What's this about torture? Get along to your bed and leave it to me. Go on; not another word; up you go." And with the kind smile which endeared him to all those with whom he came into professional contact, Henderson made his way out of the kitchen and back to the hall.

He found the others in the drawing-room where they had adjourned for coffee. Helen was seated, with Anthony and Lady Fane near her, while Kay was at the piano strumming a foxtrot with Teddy Fraser bending adoringly over her. Sir Anthony and Brent were standing near the big fire-place and the former called out to him as he entered.

"Bad cut, eh?"

Henderson went over to them.

"Cut? Oh, you mean Manning's finger? Nothing at all."

"Then where is he?" It was Brent who asked, and something in the tone of his voice made the doctor look up at him.

"He'll be here in a minute, I expect. He's conducting some experiment or other which needs periodical watching."

"And when are we going to the laboratory?" called out Kay from the piano. "Can we go now?"

"Kay, my dear..." Lady Fane rose from her seat by Helen's side. "It's getting time for us to go. The storm..."

As if taking its cue from her words the thunder rolled out again.

"Anthony," continued Lady Fane, shuddering slightly, "don't you think...?"

Kay bounced off the piano stool.

"I'm not going till I've seen the inside of that laboratory," she announced determinedly. "And who cares for a spot of thunder, anyhow? Go and fetch Mr. Manning, Hendy, and ask him if he's ready."

Brent went to the nearest window and drew back the curtain. The night was pitch dark outside.

"Doesn't look too good," remarked Teddy Fraser, peering over Brent's shoulder. "Strikes me we're in for the father of all storms. By gad! Look at that!"

A network of vivid lightning patterned the sky. Brent dropped the curtain, and as he did so the thunder pealed out in a rippling crackle which ended in a dull, heavy boom.

"The storm's coming right at us," said Brent, returning to his place at the fire-place. "Not much use our starting now, I'm afraid. Better wait a little and give it a chance to pass over."

As if to support his proposal, the thunder boomed again, and in the middle of it the door opened and Manning stepped over the threshold. The handkerchief was still wrapped about his right hand.

"We were wondering when we were going to see that experiment of yours, Mr. Manning," Kay called out to him.

Manning looked across at her.

"In five minutes, Miss Fane, all will be ready—that is, if you still care to see my laboratory." He went to a window and drew aside the curtain. The lightning flashed as he did so, and he looked back at the others with a shrug of his thin shoulders.

"I'm afraid," he said, "that you will have to put up with my hospitality a little longer. That storm we were talking about is just about to show us what it can do. Ah! Listen!"

He held up his bandaged hand and they listened to the thunder which now sounded nearer than ever. Lady Fane shuddered violently at the sound of it, and Manning fixed his smiling gaze upon her as if enjoying her agitation.

"It should do much better than that," he said, purringly. "The storm is at least five miles away as yet. It should be right over us in another half-hour." He smiled around on the others, turning then to Kay. "We might pass the time amusingly in the laboratory," he said to her. "Shall we go there now?"

"What sort of an experiment is it?" boomed Sir Anthony. "Nothing dangerous, eh?"

Manning shook his head. "Nothing dangerous at all, Sir Anthony. Merely a little exhibition of cause and effect."

He made to rub his hands together, and was reminded by the handkerchief of his cut fingers. "Shall we go, then?"

He went to the door and held it open, and after a moment's hesitation the others drifted in a body towards it, Kay in the lead.

Manning led the way across the hall to the laboratory, and, taking from his pocket a bunch of keys, he unlocked the heavy door and pushed it open, switching on the light as he entered. The others followed him into the room, passing him as he stood on one side.

When Sir Anthony and Brent, who were the last, had crossed the threshold, he swung the door to and locked it, turning a smiling face to Sir Anthony as he did so.

"A habit of mine, Sir Anthony," he said. "This room guards a number of secrets which are regarded as valuable in more than one quarter."

Chapter Eight

Still Between Ten And Eleven

THE ROOM WAS A LARGE ONE, THE WALLS OF WHICH were covered with white tiles. Around them was arranged a broad bench, and Kay gave out a delighted "Oooh!" as her eyes fell upon the complicated arrangements of chemical apparatus.

Manning crossed the room to where an imposing erection of retorts and glass tubes took up almost the whole of one side, and studied it with interest. The others looked on while he made his examination, and presently he turned to them with a smile.

"Let me explain, first of all," he said, "what the experiment has been for and the result which has been achieved." He settled himself against the bench and continued. "You have heard of the gas which has been used in warfare, no doubt," he said. "And you have probably read many a time the widely-held opinion that gas is the weapon which will decide future conflicts. The country which possesses the most deadly gas will rule the world, and this is the reason for the experiment which you are about to witness."

He cleared his throat with a rasping little cough and went on with his lecture, his half-closed eyes studying the effect of his words on each member of his audience.

"The problem of gas as a weapon in warfare," he continued, "is not so much one of finding a gas of sufficiently poisonous nature. There are very many quite deadly gases already in existence. No, the problem lies in discovering one which can be used with safety to the users as well as with danger to the enemy, and the best way to go about such a problem, is to formulate, first of all, the desired result, and then attempt to achieve it. This is what I did. Now a gas which relies upon the wind to carry it to the enemy is of questionable use, for the wind is not always so obliging an ally. A gas with a smell, or with sufficient body in it to render it visible, is also not quite one hundred per cent efficient for obvious reasons. The gas must, therefore, be odourless and invisible to start with, in addition, of course, to being poisonous. Having achieved so much, how can this be improved upon? One improvement, which immediately suggests itself, is that of delayed action. Now imagine my being desirous of killing—say, you, Mr. Fraser." Here Manning turned his half-closed eyes upon that young gentleman, who returned his gaze with an indignant stare, at the sight of which the twisted little smile on Manning's face broadened.

"With my gas," he went on, "I could achieve the result with perfect safety to myself, and with almost certain and fatal results to you. I simply call upon you at your home, or throw my gas in through your window, or send it to you through the post, or—any of a hundred methods, for my gas in its first form is liquid. I can, moreover, regulate its action to within the fraction of a minute for any time up to seventy-two hours. It is merely necessary for me to sprinkle a little of the liquid on your carpet, say, or your clothes, and at the time arranged for by me, that liquid becomes gas, and if you are anywhere within forty yards of it, you will die. In ten minutes from that time, it will have returned to its component elements, and will be no longer harmful. Thus, you can imagine, for instance, the effect upon London, say, if a fleet of aeroplanes controlled by wireless, and laden with this liquid, were to be shot down over the city? Or imagine the ease with which enemy agents could deposit quantities of it almost anywhere, and then go away before it became operative. But its methods of use can be left to other and perhaps more inventive brains. I have been concerned with the manufacture of such a gas, and tonight I am able to demonstrate to you the extent of my success."

He turned to the bench upon which was something fairly large and oblong, covered with a green baize cloth. Manning removed the cloth and revealed a glass tank, at the sight of which Helen gave a little cry and stepped forward; for inside the tank was one of Mrs. Geraint's kittens.

"Pretty little thing, is it not?" asked Manning as Helen darted forward.

"You can't kill that kitten," declared Helen, her eyes aswim with tears.

"And why not?"

"Oh, Father! To kill that little thing…"

Manning gazed at her, his mouth tight closed, his nostrils distending as he breathed.

"And again, why not?"

Tony stepped forward, followed closely by Kay whose face was white with anger.

"You are going to kill that little kitten?" she asked.

Manning smiled at her.

"I say, sir," protested Tony, "can't you get a rat, or something like that?"

"I'll smash that darned tank before I'll let you do such a thing," declared Kay, her eyes blazing. "Here, Teddy, Bill, Father, find something heavy—something I can break this wretched tank with. You can't stand by and see such cruelty."

"Manning," began Sir Anthony, "surely..."

Bill Brent stepped up to Manning and glared solemnly at him.

"I think on the whole, Manning," he said quietly, "it will be better if you find something more suitable upon which to experiment with your gas."

"He has," declared Helen. "There's a supply of rats and mice in the place somewhere."

Brent turned again to Manning. "You hear?" he said shortly. "Take that kitten out of that tank, or I will take it out for you."

"Take it out, Manning," bellowed Sir Anthony. "Dammit, man, have a heart, eh?"

"Here," said Kay, pushing Brent and Teddy Fraser, "out of my way. I'll soon settle this." She rushed to another bench and searched on it for something heavy enough for her purpose and picked up a short bar of what looked like steel. With this in her hand she returned to the glass tank before which stood Manning, who watched her with amusement.

"My dear Miss Fane," he drawled, "permit me to point out that not even the breaking of the tank can save the kitten.

The only result you are likely to achieve if you touch that tank is the death of all of us here in this room in addition to the kitten which is already doomed, for it has just a spot of my liquid upon its fur. Let me see now"—he consulted the clock hanging on the opposite wall—"The kitten is due to die in exactly two minutes."

He leaned back against the bench and smiled at the furious faces before him.

"My God! The swine!" Teddy Fraser's remark was plainly audible to all in the room, and Manning swung round on him, a low, purring chuckle coming from his throat.

"You are afraid, my friend, eh?" His head moved rapidly as he looked at the others in turn. Brent stood glaring, and in his face Manning openly sneered. Helen, with Anthony standing by her, had her hands to her throat, and her eyes, fixed as they were on her father's face, were filled with loathing. It was Henderson who broke the tension just as Teddy Fraser advanced again on Manning. He caught Fraser by the shoulder and pulled him up.

"Steady! Steady, my boy! That sort of thing can do no good." He turned to Manning. "Better let us out of here," he said soothingly. "Give me the key."

But Manning was staring beyond him at the clock. Again Henderson made his request for the key in vain. Manning's thin lips were moving silently; his eyes were fixed on the clock; he was counting the seconds. Presently his face twitched with excitement, and suddenly he turned to the tank and bent over it.

"Watch, now," he said hoarsely. "Watch the kitten…the pretty little kitten…look at its eyes, its pretty fur… See how it tries to play with my finger through the glass…pretty thing then…pretty little thing…"

His face was distorted, the eyes the merest slits; a muscle in his throat worked convulsively and from the thin mouth came the tip of his tongue, shooting in and out as it moistened the dry lips.

"Look," he whispered, "watch…watch it…"

Those in the room stared at the tank. Suddenly the kitten paused in its gambolling and clawed at the air. It fell over on its side, then jumped up to dash itself against the glass sides. Blood-flecked foam appeared around its mouth. Round and round the tank raced the tiny thing, its fur standing up on end, its head banging against the sides. Then, and it seemed, at long last, it fell over exhausted. Perhaps ten more seconds of ever feebler pawing at the air and it shuddered violently and lay still.

Slowly Manning straightened himself and turned to them. His eyes were closed completely, and on his lips was a smile of utter satisfaction. His breath came in little pants. The others stared at him in horrified silence, and presently he opened his eyes and looked furtively about him. Without a word he went to the door, produced his keys, and opened it, and one by one they filed out. Fraser, who led the way, paused opposite Manning and glared at him.

"You ought to be killed for that," he said hoarsely.

Brent who was behind him pushed him in the back and he stumbled through the door. Helen, who followed Brent, made as if to speak to her father, but words seemed to fail her, and she too stumbled blindly out into the hall. Sir Anthony with his wife went last, and words did not fail him.

"You're a damned sadist, sir," he said heavily. "I shall report this in full to the proper quarters. You're a disgrace to humanity, a...a..."

"Anthony, my dear..." Lady Fane pulled him after her through the door, and finally Manning switched the light of the laboratory off and stepped out into the hall, pulling the heavy door to and locking it behind him. He stood with his back to it, watching the others as they made their way to the drawing-room.

As the last of them disappeared through the door at the far end of the hall, he shrugged his shoulders and went in the opposite direction to his study.

And the storm, having arrived directly overhead, suddenly burst upon them, shaking the house to its foundations.

Chapter Nine

Eleven to One

SIR ANTHONY CLOSED THE DRAWING-ROOM DOOR behind him.

Helen, accompanied by the faithful and adoring Tony, had gone to the other end of the room and had sunk into a big chair. Henderson, Brent, and Fraser took up a position near the fire-place. Kay went to the piano stool, shut the piano, and leaned her arms on it.

Nobody spoke. In the presence of Helen, there was nothing that anybody could usefully say, and some of them were trying to remember exactly what they had said in her presence in the laboratory.

Outside, the storm raged, the fury of the rain on the trees and windows almost competing successfully with the continuous rumble of the thunder and being defeated only at moments of crescendo when the entire house shook.

Presently Helen rose to her feet, thrust Anthony's detaining hand away from her and walked steadily to the centre of the room.

"Listen," she said, and waited for a crash of thunder to die away before she could continue. Anthony rose to his feet and would have joined her in the centre of the room, but she waved him back.

"No, please, Tony. Stay where you are."

She fought for control of herself.

"I don't know what to say to you…"

"Helen!" Anthony made a step towards her, but again she waved him back.

"I…I think that perhaps I had better say nothing," she continued. "You have seen for yourselves. You must stay here until the storm has passed. You…you can't go out in this, can you? I…I just wanted to say that when you go, please forget all about me and tonight…the engagement, and… and everything. There is no question, Tony, of my keeping you to your promise…"

In three strides Anthony was at her side and had taken her in his arms.

"Helen, my darling, you mustn't talk like that," he said earnestly. "That's all tommy rot. Tomorrow, or as soon as we can get away, you are coming with us, d'you hear? And we're going to be married straight away. You need never come back here."

For a moment she seemed content to stay in his arms, then she pressed with her hands against him, pushing him away.

"Tony, you don't know what you're saying. You can't, my dear, you can't… Don't you see? He's mad…insane…"

Anthony stepped back from her, his face horror-stricken.

"And I… I am his daughter," she finished.

"Now d'you see?" she continued presently. "But I swear on my honour to you all"—she looked around at the others—"that I did not know it until tonight. I have never seen him like this before…"

Kay ran to her side and put her arm about her.

"You're talking through your hat, old thing," she said with a brave imitation of lightness. "Let's go upstairs and pop into bed. Come along, Helen. Pull yourself together."

Kay tried to urge Helen to the door, and Henderson came to her help.

"That's a splendid idea," he said. "You go up to bed. You've been through quite enough for one day. We can talk this out in the morning. Go now, Helen."

She clung to him.

"Hendy," she pleaded, "if… Will you take me away from here tomorrow?"

The doctor nodded his head. "Yes, of course, my dear. Don't you worry, we'll fix up something."

Helen gave him a grateful look and allowed herself to be led to the door. Suddenly Anthony rushed after her.

"Helen… Helen…what d'you take me for? D'you think I'd allow this to make any difference?"

Sir Anthony cleared his throat and came out of a reverie.

"I should hope not, by gad! I should damned well hope not. We'll talk it all over in the morning."

Henderson went with Kay and Helen to see them up to the latter's room.

"Good God!" boomed Sir Anthony as the door closed behind Helen, Kay, and the doctor. "Good God, sir! Good God!"

"Anthony, my dear…" bleated Lady Fane, and went and sat down on the nearest chair. She began to weep silently.

"I knew it from the first," declared Teddy. "Of course he's mad; mad as a hatter, and of all the appalling swines I've ever bumped up against! And to think of that poor kid living here alone with him all these years. No wonder she looked like she did. Well, I'm…"

"Look here, you people,"—Anthony turned from the door at which he had been staring ever since it had closed behind Helen and the other two—"let's chuck talking about it. The question is, what are we to do now? We can't go home in this, and in any case, we can't leave Helen here alone in the house with that madman. What shall we do about it?"

"Stay here." Bill Brent made his first contribution to the conversation since the return from the laboratory. "I suggest that Sir Anthony and Lady Fane go to bed—or go to lie down, anyhow. Henderson knows the house inside out, and he can fix up a bedroom; and Tony, Teddy, and myself can stay down here. It won't do us any harm, and I agree with Anthony, we can't go home in this. Better get off early in the morning, and take Helen with us. What d'you say, sir?"

Sir Anthony turned it over in his mind.

"Well," he growled presently, "I suppose there is nothing else for us to do. Question is, can we find bedrooms for ourselves?"

"Henderson will do that for you, sir. There's no sense in us all staying up down here."

The doctor came back into the room, and Brent immediately put the suggestion to him.

"Excellent idea," he agreed. "I'll find bedrooms for all of you, and there's not even any need for anybody to stay down here. This storm is going to last for some time, and some sleep won't harm any of us. Manning won't trouble us again tonight. Come with me, Lady Fane, and you too, Sir Anthony."

They bade the other three good night and went with the doctor.

"Well, if the doc can fix me up with a room, not all the lunatics in the world are going to get between me and a good night's rest. I'm all used up." Brent stretched himself and found a cigarette which he lit.

Silence ensued, and each became busy with his own thoughts. Each had plenty to say but there seemed no point in saying it. They were, in fact, suffering from the reaction from the excitement of the evening. Henderson returned presently and took all three of them upstairs, distributing them amongst the adequate supply of bedrooms. Then he himself found a room, entered it, and carefully locked the door behind him.

Downstairs the light continued to burn in Manning's study, and towards one o'clock, it was the only light in the house. By it, Manning himself continued to sit at the table and stare down at the open album on his table.

It was not until a clock in the room struck one, that Manning switched off the light and turned his chair towards the window so that he could watch the storm, and think— and wait.

Chapter Ten

One to Three Forty-Five

It was two o'clock before the storm began to show signs of dying down. Kay, who was occupying one of the twin beds in Helen's room, had not slept at all. Her mind had been too busily at work on the events of the night to allow her to do so, and she lay quietly in the darkness, listening to Helen's regular breathing and going over and over again the experiences of the dinner and what followed.

This was not the only thing Kay had to think about. Teddy had managed to slip in another two eloquent proposals during the evening, and although Kay had turned him down with her usual flippant scorn and laughter, she was rapidly coming to the conclusion that, sooner or later, she would have to treat the matter seriously and persuade Teddy to accept her as a sister. For marry Teddy Fraser she could not dream of doing unless something drastic happened to Bill Brent; in which case she might accept Teddy merely because there would no longer be much point in hurting him, which she hated doing.

Kay was in love with Bill Brent. She had fought bitterly against it for over a month, but it was no good continuing the unequal fight, and she surrendered without further ado.

As she lay there in the darkness Kay wondered what the end of it was going to be. She harboured absolutely no illusions about herself. She did not even consider that her violent Eton crop was an inducement to Bill's favourable regard. On the contrary, she had excellent reason to believe that he looked upon her particular method of wearing her hair as a mild form of insanity, which she would probably grow out of as she got to know the world a little better. Her habit of doing violence to her eyelids with green paint and to her fingernails with stains of all colours from black up to a snappy crimson caused Bill, she knew, a good deal of wondering amusement. And yet, she continued to indulge these adolescent foibles. Why? Why, for goodness' sake, couldn't she allow her hair to grow and throw away her bits and pieces of paints?

Kay had often asked herself these very questions. She really wanted to do so, and the only reason why she didn't, that she could think of, was the memory of a certain occasion when Bill, himself, had once asked her if she thought going about like she did, made her less difficult to look at? She had politely told him to go to the devil, and the very next day had almost had her Eton crop bleached just to see what he would think of to say to that. No, she just could not bring herself to appear pleasing in Bill's sight. Silly? Probably. In fact, without a doubt, idiotic in the extreme, but perhaps she was an idiot, which explained it. In any case, she would see Mr. Bill Brent sizzling in the nether regions before she came all over fluffy and feminine just to please him. Not that she didn't love him to death. She did, and, whereas she would cheerfully have laid her life down for him at a moment's notice, and at the slightest hint from him that such a course of action on her part would help him, she would not grow her hair for him, nor would she refrain from smoking gaspers out of foot-long holders, nor from painting her eyes, nails—toe as well as finger—any darned colour she liked.

So there it was. Life was a funny thing altogether. Why, she wondered, did fate have to fill her, of all people, with an unrequited passion? Why could she not have loved Teddy who thought her Eton crop and painted eyes the last words in beauty? Why couldn't...?

She sat up in bed suddenly. Was that something outside her door, or... Yes, there it was again, a soft, padding noise.

Kay listened for a moment, and then slipped out of bed in the dark. She crept to the door and listened again, her hand on the knob, and, hearing nothing, she opened the door carefully and peered out. She nearly slammed it to again as she caught a glimpse of something white flitting along the corridor towards the top of the stairs.

But Kay was made of stern stuff, and instead of shutting the door and diving straight beneath the bedclothes, she opened it still wider and even went so far as to creep out on to the corridor.

The figure in white was nearing the top of the stairs. It reached them and commenced the descent. Without thinking, Kay darted silently in pursuit and arrived at the stairs when the figure was half-way down them.

It was a woman. It couldn't be her mother, for she was half the size of this one. Helen, she had left in bed. One of the maids? Mrs. Geraint, of course! But what was she doing walking about the house at this time of night? Going to make herself a cup of tea, perhaps? At the very thought of a cup of tea, Kay perched herself expertly on the banisters and made a swift and entirely silent descent, arriving at the bottom just as the figure was turning into the hall and towards the kitchen.

"Mrs. Geraint," whispered Kay.

The figure paused.

"Mrs. Geraint," whispered Kay again, and this time the figure turned and came slowly towards her. Something in her curiously rigid way of walking made Kay pause before speaking again, and she waited until the other came right up to her. Then she had a shock.

Mrs. Geraint it was, all right; and Mrs. Geraint with her eyes wide open but unseeing. Sleep-walking! Of course! Helen had told Kay something once about Mrs. Geraint sleep-walking.

She dodged silently out of the oncoming housekeeper's way and trembled as the walker cannoned into the banisters at the foot of the stairs, fearful lest she would awake. Kay had a hazy idea that sleep-walkers who were awakened suddenly had fits, or died, or something, and she almost sighed with relief as Mrs. Geraint turned away from the banisters and continued her serene way down the hall to the door at the rear of it. She disappeared through it, and Kay was about to follow when a movement in the shadows away to her left caught her eye. She strained her eyes in that direction and stifled a cry as a figure stepped out into the centre of the hall. It came steadily towards her and she crouched back against the wall, her hand pressed to her mouth. Then she nearly fainted with amazement and relief. It was Teddy.

"Teddy," she whispered, and the figure gave a little jump.

"Who the..." came from it in a hoarse whisper.

"It's me, Kay."

"Kay!"

"Yes, Kay, you fathead! What are you doing down here?"

"Where are you?"

Mr. Fraser approached her where she stood in the shadows and peered down at her.

"So it is!" he whispered. "Well, I'm damned! And for the love of Mike, who was the spook?"

"Mrs. Geraint sleep-walking."

"Good-gracious-to-goodness!"

"Sh-sh!"

The warning came from Kay in a little hiss, and she pointed to the kitchen door.

"Here she comes again," she whispered. "Look out!"

Teddy ranged himself alongside her against the wall and together they watched the white-robed figure of the house-keeper pad its way across the hall towards them as they stood near the foot of the stairs.

As she came nearer they noticed that there was a knife—a large, white-handled carving knife in her right hand and that she held it as if it were a dagger. At the foot of the stairs she paused for a moment, then turned away in the direction of the dining-room. They allowed her to get some six paces ahead and then followed. She led them into the dining-room where she laid the knife carefully on the table. Then she turned to the door again, went through it and across the hall to the stairs which she proceeded to mount.

Kay and Teddy watched her go up and take the corridor to her room.

"That's that," whispered Teddy. "She's gone back to her room. Let's go and sit down somewhere."

They went into the drawing-room and sat down in the dark.

"Now," said Kay, still speaking in a whisper, "what were you doing down in the hall, Teddy?"

"Trying to get into the laboratory."

"What on earth for?"

"Couldn't sleep thinking about those darned cats. Thought I'd have a shot at letting them out."

"But how on earth did you expect to get into the laboratory?"

"Pick the lock, of course, you mutt."

"And didn't you?"

"No. Couldn't do it."

"Mutt yourself then."

They continued to sit in silence. Then:

"I say, Kay."

"Yes?"

"I say, old thing, I really am most completely crazy about you."

Kay leaned her head on his shoulder, and he put his arm around her, holding her gently, so that she could not slip. For long moments he enjoyed in silence the sensation of supporting her, then he came to the attack again.

"I say, Kay, why the deuce can't we get married and have

done with it? I can't sleep, or eat, or enjoy a cigarette even. Have a heart, old thing, eh?"

Kay sighed, and something in the sigh made him bend his head to see her face. Then he cursed fluently and quietly under his breath. For Kay had suddenly taken it into her head to go to sleep.

And in less than ten minutes, Mr. Fraser joined her in the land of dreams.

Chapter Eleven

One to Three Forty-Five (Continued)

IN THE STUDY WERE TWO MEN. ONE OF THEM LAY sprawled across the big writing-table with the white handle of a big carving-knife sticking out of his back between his shoulder blades. The other, who wore over the lower half of his face a dark scarf, was on his knees at the side of the table, working feverishly with his gloved hands at the drawers in it.

The pulling of the drawers seemed to trouble him, for he would first feel beneath them with great care before attempting to withdraw them. When he was satisfied, he would pull out the drawer and empty the contents on to the floor, scanning the papers as they fell with the aid of a little electric torch. Presently, he turned his attention to the body of the dead man.

Here again he worked methodically, first emptying each pocket in turn of its contents. Once, when he had to get at the breast pocket of the coat, he was compelled to stretch across the body until his face touched the dead head. He shuddered slightly, but did not withdraw his hand until it was filled with the contents of the pocket.

These he laid down on the floor, scanning each with the utmost care. One of them, a tiny notebook, he seized on eagerly and opened its pages. Page after page he turned over until, at last, he gave a sigh of relief. He had found what he wanted.

With uncanny absence of sound, he rose to his feet and glided to the wall beyond the desk. In it was fitted a safe, and with one more glance at the open page of the little book, he took it between his teeth, slipping it beneath the lower end of the scarf to do so, and then he commenced work on the dial in the front of the safe.

More references to the little book, and after each one a return to the dial; delicate fingering, then the nod of his head as he heard the faint click; until, at last, it was finished. The final turn, and the safe would be open.

He slipped the little book into his pocket and concentrated on the safe. Working with his face close to the dial, he made the turn, and heard the click. Then something squirted out and caught him full in the face.

He stepped back with a stifled little cry of surprise and pain. For the stuff, whatever it was, had hit his face just above the top of the scarf and was running down his cheek and nose inside; and it burned with a curious tingling sensation.

Burn? That wasn't the word for it. The stuff ate into his face, biting its way through his flesh. He put his hands up, nudged the scarf up into his eyes, and screamed.

Agony! Searing, white-hot agony! Something tearing at his face, biting, burning...

He staggered back against a chair and turned it over. With outstretched hands, for he was blind with this stuff, whatever it was, he stumbled forward.

His hands struck something—glass, for through his agony he heard it crash to the gravel outside. He must get out somehow. He screamed again, mad with the pain, and pushed his way blindly through the windows. He was outside. He felt the rain fall with a hard rush on to his upturned face. About him the air filled with the deafening crash of thunder and with the flash of lightning which he, now blind, could not see.

He staggered on, a low groan tearing from his throat, and time and again he stumbled. Another ear-splitting crash of thunder, and then something hit him on the back of his head and the agony left him.

Behind him, in the house he had just left, Bill Brent was hurrying down the stairs.

BOOK TWO

Chapter One

Four a.m. to Five

"Why, God bless my soul!"

Bill Brent, his arms full of Helen's dead weight, paused on his way across the hall and looked up. Sir Anthony, fully dressed, was hurrying down the stairs, his booming voice shattering the quiet of the house as he came.

"Brent? Good God, sir! What's happened here?"

"It's Helen, Sir Anthony. She's fainted. Open that door behind you."

Sir Anthony bustled to the drawing-room door, opened it, and switched on the light.

"Good God, sir!" he boomed again as he stood on the threshold, and Brent, coming up beside him, saw the sleeping forms of Kay and Teddy Fraser on the settee across the room.

At the sound of her father's voice Kay awoke with a jerk and sat up. Teddy came to with equal suddenness and rubbed his eyes.

"What are you doing down here, Kay?" Sir Anthony boomed on. "Fraser... God bless my soul!"

Brent stepped past him towards the settee from which Kay and Teddy arose as he approached, and they watched in open-eyed silence as he laid the unconscious form of Helen upon it.

"Am I still asleep?" asked Kay, as he straightened himself.

Brent turned his eyes on her. Something in them brought a sudden flush to her face, a flush which deepened at the tone of his voice as he replied.

"Sorry to disturb you," he said, "but as you see, Helen has fainted." He looked towards the door as Henderson entered. "Here's Hendy," he continued. "Help him look after Helen."

"Bu-but what's happened?" stammered Kay. "I left Helen asleep in our room just now..."

"Just now?"

"Yes. Just after one."

"And you've been down here ever since?"

"Ever since?"

"It's four o'clock."

Kay and Teddy stared at each other in amazement.

"Look here, Bill..." began Teddy, when Sir Anthony's voice filled the room and drowned him.

"What's the meaning of all this, eh? Brent walking about with Helen in a faint; Kay sleeping on the settee with young Fraser; what the devil does it all mean, eh? Where's Manning?"

Henderson, who was bending over Helen, looked up at the irate speaker.

"Please!" he said in his gentle voice. "Not quite so loud, Sir Anthony. Kay, my dear, go and get me some water, and, if you have them, some smelling salts."

For a moment Kay fixed her eyes on Brent's, then, without a word, she turned and ran from the room.

"Now then," continued Sir Anthony, soothing his voice into a sort of minor bellow, "perhaps somebody will explain all this. Fraser, what were you doing down here asleep with Kay? And what, sir,"—turning to Brent—"were you doing carrying Helen about in a faint?"

Teddy Fraser shifted uneasily from one foot to another. Brent looked down at Henderson who was studying anxiously the pale face of the unconscious girl.

Sir Anthony got no immediate answer to his questions, and was about to speak again, when a plaintive whimper from the door made them all look round. Lady Fane was entering the room with quick, nervous steps.

"Anthony, my dear…" she said as she came forward, and then, as she saw the form of Helen lying on the settee. "Helen…my dear…" She ran the remaining steps to the settee and bent over it.

"Helen's fainted," explained Sir Anthony, "and I'll be damned if any of 'em will explain themselves. Where's Manning?"

"Sir Anthony"—Brent's voice was grave and quiet— "something has happened. Helen has had a pretty bad shock."

He tried to make signs to prevent the baronet pressing his questions in the presence of his wife, but it was no good.

"I tell you," he boomed, more loudly than ever, "that I insist on knowing. What has happened? What the devil is all this about?"

Brent sighed heavily. Then, as it occurred to him that they would all have to know sooner or later, he spoke.

"Manning is dead," he said.

"Dead?" For once Sir Anthony spoke in a whisper.

"But Bill…my dear…" Lady Fane came and placed a hand on his sleeve.

"That was the shock Helen had." Brent turned away from them and walked towards the window. He was turning over in his mind the advisability of telling them everything.

"Dead, eh?"

Brent turned as Sir Anthony spoke again, and saw Kay come quickly into the room, her hands laden with bottles and a glass of water. She stopped short at the sound of her father's voice, her face suddenly pale.

"Dead?" she said, horror in her voice. "Helen…"

"Manning," explained her father shortly. "Brent says he's dead."

Kay gave vent to a great sigh, and a bottle fell to the floor from her hands.

"I… I thought for a moment you meant Helen," she said, and brought the water and the remainder of her burden to the settee. "Here you are, Hendy," she went on, "here's three sorts of salts. Hasn't she come to yet? Poor old Helen!" She knelt by the settee and, taking one of Helen's hands between her own, commenced to chafe it.

"How did he die?" Sir Anthony's voice had recovered, and was no longer a whisper.

"What does it matter as long as he's dead?" Kay put her question without looking up.

"Kay…my dear…" Lady Fane's voice was filled with horror. "How can you? He's dead."

"Well? And isn't that the best bit of news we've heard since we came here this evening?" Kay continued her vigorous chafing as she spoke. "Who cares what's happened to him anyhow? Look at poor Helen here. Hendy, do something, old thing, do something." She gave the doctor, who was kneeling at her side, a prod with her fist. "She looks as if she's dying. She's not even breathing. Hendy, can't you…?"

"Steady, Kay!" Henderson's voice was quiet and calm. "There's nothing like that to worry about. Helen will be all right presently. If you've got a handkerchief, dip it in that water and bathe her head. And," he added as she fumbled for a handkerchief, "keep calm, old girl. There'll be lots for you to do presently." He busied himself with the bottles and the others, their attention thus brought to the death-like face on the settee, stood around and watched him anxiously.

"Doctor Henderson…my dear…" Lady Fane went down on one knee at his side. "Wouldn't she be better in bed?" She laid a gentle hand on the unconscious girl's forehead. "She's terribly cold."

"All in good time," replied the doctor soothingly. "We'll get Bill to carry her up just as soon as ever she shows signs of coming to."

"It's so long for a faint…" Lady Fane was clearly not satisfied, and the others pressed closer as they heard Henderson's reply.

"It's more than a faint," he explained. "She's had a terrible shock, poor child." He stretched out one hand, and they watched him raise one of his patient's eyelids. His face grew anxious as he turned to those standing about the settee. "She'll come to in a minute," he said. "Could one of you go and tell somebody to put one or two hot-water bottles in her bed. Better get…" he was about to say "Mrs. Geraint," when he remembered what he had seen but a few minutes before.

"I know Mrs. Geraint's room," said Kay jumping up. "I'll go and wake her."

She made for the door and turned back as Brent called out after her.

"Wake Anthony at the same time," he said, "and tell him to come down."

She glanced at him coldly, nodded, and went. They heard her running swiftly up the stairs. And it seemed to Bill Brent that, hardly had those pattering footsteps died away when they came running down the stairs again and into the room. With the others, he turned to the door as Kay appeared there, her eyes wide with fright.

"Come up, somebody," she said. "Tony's…" As she spoke she turned and ran up the stairs again so that they did not catch what she was saying. Bill Brent ran after her, closely followed by Teddy Fraser and, more slowly, by Sir Anthony.

Brent was the first to follow Kay into Tony's room, and he found her on her knees, tugging at the knotted sheets which bound him to a chair. His mouth was gagged, and tied round with a towel from beneath which trickled a thin stream of blood.

In a few seconds Brent had loosened the knots of the sheets that bound him, and Tony staggered to his feet and pulled the towel from his face and the gag from his mouth. For a moment he swayed where he stood and surveyed them drunkenly, the blood still flowing from his lip which was badly cut.

"That…that…swine Strange," he muttered. "He…he dotted me one…just lemme get at him…"

He tottered forward a few steps, then suddenly pulled himself together and passed a hand over his eyes. Then, with a shake of his head, he pushed his way through them and made for the door. They followed him along the corridor and down the stairs, and as they neared the foot, Brent heard a voice he knew was Helen's. It was raised in a frightened scream.

"Don't let him come near me...keep back, Father... Keep him back, somebody... Tony Tony..."

Tony cleared the remaining six stairs in a bound and Brent followed him. Together they rushed into the drawing-room. Henderson was pressing Helen back on to the settee; Lady Fane was standing by her husband, wringing her hands and crying.

The doctor looked up as the other came hurrying into the room.

"Quiet, please," he said. "Bill, come and carry her upstairs for me—in a minute."

They gathered around the settee, Brent holding Tony back as he made to kneel down at its side. Helen had sunk back on to the cushions and was breathing in short, spasmodic gasps. Presently she opened terror-stricken, unseeing eyes, and from her lips came a stream of babbled words.

"Father... Father...keep away from me... I hate you, d'you hear?... I hate you...hate you...all my life... My mother... what did you do to her?... Don't come near me...keep away...keep him away, somebody... Tony, my darling... come to me..."

In spite of the restraining hands of the doctor, she struggled to a sitting position and shrank back against the cushions, her face distorted with terror, her eyes distended, her hands raised as if defending her face.

"I hate you...hate you..." she babbled on, "d'you hear? I hate you...hate you..." Suddenly the tenseness of her body relaxed, and in her delirium she commenced to cry quietly, the tears streaming from her eyes. "I... I...love you, Tony, darling," she went on brokenly. "Take me away from him... take me away..."

She sank back, limp and exhausted. The lids of her eyes, from which the tears continued to flow, closed, and the doctor took his hands away from her and sighed heavily.

"That's better," he said. "I wanted to see those tears. Now, Bill...upstairs with her."

But Tony pushed Brent's restraining hand away and bending over the settee, put his arms about the limp form and lifted it up. Then, preceded by the doctor, he made his way to the door.

Chapter Two

Four a.m. to Five (Continued)

"Now, sir."

Sir Anthony turned to Brent when, Kay and Lady Fane having followed the others upstairs, they were alone.

"Now, sir. What does all this mean? First of all I find you carrying Helen across the hall. Then I find my daughter asleep in here with young Fraser. Then you tell me Manning is dead, and finally Tony rushes in here with his face all cut about, and what I naturally want to know is, sir, what the devil does it all mean, eh? Come on. Out with it, Brent. Why, damme…"

Brent waved a hand wearily and sat down. There were many things that he, too, wanted to know the meaning of.

What, for instance, had Kay been doing asleep with Fraser in the drawing-room? She had gone up to bed before him last night and, as she had said herself, it had been one o'clock when she had fallen asleep. Then what, exactly…? He pulled himself up sharply. What was he thinking? There had been moments, lately, when he had thought he had caught a look in Kay's eyes when their eyes had met—a look entirely at variance with the usual gleam of mischief, a look which contrasted oddly with the absurd Eton crop, the painted eyelids, the glaring colour of the lips; a look which had stirred something deep in his heart. Why, in any case, should the discovery of her alone and asleep with Fraser in the drawing-room, in the early hours of the morning, have suddenly filled him with such amazed anger and bitterness? Was it not just the sort of idiotic thing Kay was famous for doing? Had not Kay almost ceased to surprise both him and everybody else with her ridiculous behaviour? He was a fool to worry about it; he was something worse to have thought, even for a moment, as he had.

What, too, was Sir Anthony doing ready dressed at that time of the morning? How did Helen creep unawares upon them in the study, and where had she come from? Not from the drawing-room, for Kay had said that she had left Helen asleep in bed. And finally, what on earth had happened to Tony? Where did Strange come into it, unless he was the author of the noises in the study which had brought Brent out of bed in the first instance?

His head commenced to ache. Sir Anthony, with a noisy sigh, found a chair and sat down heavily. Brent looked up at his employer.

"I don't know what half of it all means, Sir Anthony," he said. "I went to bed last night just after you others, and I was awakened by noises."

"What sort of noises?"

"I heard a scream of sorts, and the sound of breaking glass. I came downstairs and went to the study which is directly underneath my room, for I was certain the sounds had come from there, and I found Manning dead."

"In the study?"

Brent nodded.

"In the study. Henderson had been disturbed too, and he got there almost as soon as I did." Brent paused as he remembered something else. "Yes," he continued, "that reminds me. We saw Mrs. Geraint sleep-walking—at least Henderson said she was walking in her sleep."

"Good God!" Sir Anthony puffed out his cheeks. "Mrs. Geraint sleep-walking now. What next, eh?"

"She went up the stairs to her room," Brent continued, "and I went into the study. Manning was dead—murdered."

Sir Anthony shot out of his chair.

"Eh? What's that? Murdered? Whom by? Eh?"

"God knows. The windows were open and one of them was broken—the sounds of breaking glass that I heard, I suppose. Somebody must have rushed through them and screamed for some reason or other. I would have gone out to look for him, but the storm was too much of a good thing."

Sir Anthony sat down in his chair again.

"Murdered, eh? Murdered, you said?"

"Stabbed through the back with a carving knife."

Having got over his first surprise, Sir Anthony became the man of action.

"What about the police?" he asked. "We'd better let them know. Come on, Brent, pull yourself together man. Where's the telephone?"

"Bust." Brent passed a hand over his head. "Lightning, I expect, unless whoever did it cut the wire first. Can't get through, anyhow. And that reminds me."

He rose quickly to his feet and made for the door.

"Where are you going to, Brent?" Sir Anthony made as if to follow him, but Brent waved him back.

"Sit here, sir, and wait for the others," he said. "There's something I forgot all about."

Without waiting for more, Brent passed through the doorway and ran up the stairs three at a time. Arrived at the top, he hurried along the corridor, past his own door, to the room next to his which he knew to be Manning's.

The door was unlocked, and he turned the knob stepped inside, and pressed the light switch. The buzzing sound which he had heard on first waking, and which he remembered thinking had come from this room, was still going on.

He looked around the room curiously. It was barely furnished; just a large, double bed, a chair or two, a wardrobe, and what looked like a wireless set placed by the side of the bed. It was from this last that the buzzing sound was coming, and Brent stepped towards it.

It was a shallow cabinet in the face of which were a number of switches and a slot divided up into squares and covered with frosted glass. With each short buzz one of the squares lit up, and Brent read the word "Study" painted upon the glass in black lettering. Undoubtedly, a burglar alarm of some sort. Probably, Brent thought, Manning had been awakened by this contraption, had gone down to the study, and met his death at the hands of the intruder there.

He played about with the switch beneath the lighted square, pressing it down, and the buzzing stopped. At the same time, the light behind the square went out.

Brent looked about the room. There seemed to be nothing in it which had been disturbed in any way; nothing which might, in the words of the detective novel, tell a story, or provide a clue. Even the bed was undisturbed, and had obviously not been slept in.

Not been slept in! Brent's eyes opened wide as they rested on the bed. Manning, then, had not been to bed, and could not, therefore, have been disturbed by his burglar alarm. He probably had not even been in the room when it made its alarm, unless he had spent the night up to nearly four o'clock in the morning sitting up in one of the chairs—an unlikely circumstance, for the only chairs there were of the high-backed variety. No, any man in his senses waiting in that room for some hours, would have done his waiting lying down on the bed, and nobody had lain in this bed. Furthermore, would he not—had he been in the room at the time—have silenced his alarm before proceeding to the study to investigate?

Brent stepped to the uncovered windows and looked out into the darkness of the night. The rain was still coming down with tropical heaviness, making a thunderous roar as it beat upon the trees and the ground outside.

Suddenly the darkness of the night disappeared before a vivid flash of lightning, and Brent drew in his breath with a sharp hiss, for, in the second of time during which the lightning had lit up the night with vivid brightness, he had seen something—the figure of a man lying on the ground not fifty yards away from the house. Something—it had looked like a branch of a tree—lay across him.

Brent turned from the room and hurried downstairs. He arrived in the drawing-room just in time to hear Sir Anthony announce to the others, who had returned there, the news of the murder.

"...that's what Brent said," Sir Anthony was saying in his impressive voice. "Manning was murdered, stabbed."

Brent burst into the room in the middle of the silence which followed this announcement.

"Hendy," he said hurriedly. "There's somebody—a man—outside in the grounds. One of you had better come with me."

He went back into the hall and hurried across it to the study. The others followed close upon his heels, and pressed upon him as he unlocked the study door. He turned to them, and saw Kay and Lady Fane behind the three men, waiting for him to open the door.

"Take Kay and Lady Fane back to the drawing-room," he ordered. "There's no need for them to come in here."

He waited until Sir Anthony and the doctor, the former with loud-voiced authority, the latter with gentle persuasion, were conducting the two ladies back to the drawing-room before he opened the door and, followed by Tony and Teddy, both of whom gasped as they did so, he entered the room and crossed it to the broken windows.

He pulled them open and the full force of the storm burst upon them as they stood just inside the room.

"We'll have to shut these windows," said Brent. "You, Teddy, stay here and open them for us when we come back. Tony, come with me and help me carry him, whoever he may be. We'll have to dash for it. It's right opposite here, and there's nothing between us and it. Now then!"

He charged out through the windows, followed by Tony, and together they ran across the lawn in the direction Brent had indicated. A welcome flash of lightning gave them a sight of the man not six yards ahead, and they slowed down to a walk and carefully felt their way forward.

A heavy branch of a tree had fallen across the man who lay quite still, and, working in the dark, aided at minute intervals by the frequent lightning, they succeeded at last in moving the branch and drawing the man from beneath it. Brent slipped his arms beneath the man's shoulders while Tony took his feet, and thus they struggled slowly back to the lighted windows where Teddy, accompanied now by Sir Anthony and the doctor, was waiting to let them in.

Brent, walking backwards and carrying the head and shoulders, entered the lighted room first, and as he stepped through the open windows, Teddy Fraser, who was standing ready to close them, bent forward.

"My God!" he said in a horrified voice. "Look at his face! It's Strange, the butler. But look at his face. Oh, my God! I've never seen anything so awful."

He turned away, his own face like chalk, and closed the windows as Tony, soaked to the skin, stepped into the room.

Chapter Three

Five to Six

BRENT AND TONY LAID THEIR BURDEN ON THE FLOOR, and all five shuddered as they looked down on it.

The scarf had been torn away from the face, one side of which was horribly burnt. Blood still flowed from the mouth which was twisted into a grin of agony.

Henderson went down on his knees and opened the coat and vest. The others watched while he slipped one hand beneath the clothing. Presently he looked up and announced in his quiet voice:

"He's alive still. Help me with his clothes, one of you."

For a moment nobody responded to the command, then Brent, feeling suddenly sick, dropped on his knees beside the doctor and helped to remove coat and vest. Then Tony, swallowing hard, knelt too and lent a hand, and in a few minutes they had stripped the man to the waist. Then they got to their feet and stood silently watching the doctor as he passed investigating hands over the pitiful body.

"Ribs," Henderson said presently. "As I thought, his ribs

are crushed in. He's dying, and I'm afraid there's nothing that I can do for him. I haven't even a hypodermic here with me in case he comes to."

"Poor devil!" muttered Brent. "Must have been that branch of tree which he was lying under."

He fell silent again, watching the doctor as the latter examined the burned face.

"That's vitriol," the doctor said presently, "and unless I'm very much mistaken, I know where it came from."

He rose to his feet and went over to the safe, the dial on which he examined carefully.

"Yes," he said again, presently. "It's from this thing here." He pointed to the face of the safe, and Brent joined him there. "This was one of Manning's little ideas," continued the doctor. "He told me about it once. The front of this safe is false, and this dial affair here contains vitriol which squirted out when the dial was turned in the right way."

"Good God!" Sir Anthony shuddered violently. "Then this fellow here came to steal something, eh?"

"Looks like it."

"Well, poor devil, he got what he asked for then. Good God, what a punishment!"

Henderson returned to the side of the unconscious man and bent over him again. Brent turned from his study of the safe, and as he did so, his right foot struck against something on the floor. It was a small clock which might have fallen from the table, and he bent down and picked it up, turning it over in his hands as he straightened himself. The glass was broken, and a piece of it had got wedged in underneath the hands which pointed to twenty to two. He shook it gently, and the piece of glass fell to the floor. Instantly the clock commenced to tick, and Brent stared at it with sudden curiosity.

"Here's a funny thing," he said presently to the others who looked up at the sound of his voice. "This clock must have fallen from the table." He paused, thinking hard.

"Well, what about it?" Sir Anthony asked.

"It stopped—I mean it must have stopped when it fell and broke the glass. A bit of it got wedged in the hands, and now that I've shaken it out, it's going again." Again he paused, and once more Sir Anthony had to prompt him.

"Yes? Well, what's funny in that?"

"It stopped at twenty to two," continued Brent.

For a moment there was silence in the room as the others considered this information. Then Tony spoke.

"You mean it must have been twenty to two when Manning…"

"Was murdered," Brent finished for him. "Unless the clock was slow or something."

"Let's have a look at it." Tony came to Brent's side and looked at the little clock in the other's hands. "It wasn't slow yesterday afternoon when I was here," he said presently. "I remember that clock perfectly. I spent quite a lot of time looking at it as I was talking to Manning."

Brent put the clock down on the table and stared down at the dead man. Presently, he stretched out one hand and touched the dead hand which lay across the papers. He withdrew it instantly.

"I say, Hendy," he said, and then, as the doctor looked up. "If Manning was killed at about four, just before you and I came down here, would he be stone cold now?"

The doctor rose stiffly to his feet and came to the table. He, too, touched the hand and the face of the dead man. His eyes wandered to the pool of blood which lay on the floor beneath the body, and he bent down for a closer look at the body, peering at the bloodstains about the mouth. Brent watched him eagerly as he straightened himself.

"How long would you say he's been dead?" he asked.

Henderson thought for a moment before replying.

"I can't say with any sort of exactness without a proper examination of the body," he said presently. "But he's certainly been dead for a lot more than an hour."

"More like three or four hours, eh?"

The doctor nodded his head.

"So Strange must have been here with the body for some time, then?"

"But I saw Strange upstairs just before four." They all turned to Anthony as he spoke. "Twenty to four, as a matter of fact, for I remember looking at the clock in my bedroom."

"Where was he then?"

"I was sitting up in my room," explained Anthony. "I couldn't sleep after last night's business. I just sat down and thought about it. Then I heard something outside my room, and I went to have a look to see what it was. It was Strange creeping down the corridor, and as soon as he saw me he put his finger to his mouth and came up to me. He asked me in a whisper if he could have a word with me, so I took him into my room, and just as I turned round to him, he dotted me one and knocked me clean out. When I came to, he had me half-trussed up with a filthy gag in my mouth. That was at twenty to four, and I'm certain he was coming from his room when I saw him first."

"Then he must have come down before, and gone back to his room for something," said Brent. "Curious!"

Very curious, he thought, as the doctor returned to his position at the side of the man on the floor. If there was anything in his idea that Manning had been killed at the time the clock had stopped, then Strange must have stayed in the house with his dead victim, and even walked about upstairs two hours afterwards. Would any man commit such a murder as this and have the nerve to stay near the body for three hours in a house full of people?

A movement of the doctor interrupted his thoughts. Henderson was bending still lower over the man, his face set in concentration. Brent joined the others and watched.

Presently he saw one eyelid—the one which was not burned—flicker faintly, and there was a slight movement of the lips. They stood and watched in silence as the movements in the face became gradually more pronounced. Then, at last, the one uninjured eye opened, and the writhing lips parted. Something like a sob came from Teddy Fraser, at the sound of which the doctor looked up with a frown and raised one hand.

"Be quiet," he said, and turned his attention again to the dying man.

It seemed a long time before anything more happened. Actually it was a matter of seconds, at the end of which a whispered groan came from the ground. Brent dropped onto one knee. Strange, his face now working convulsively, seemed to be trying to speak. The doctor stretched out a hand and touched the forehead.

"All right," he said soothingly. "Take it easy."

But the face continued to work harder. There came

another deep groan, stronger this time, from the tortured lips, and then they could both see and hear the breath come in short, painful gasps.

"He's trying to say something," muttered Brent. "My God, Hendy, isn't there anything you can do for him?"

As if he understood, Strange turned his one eye on Brent, and for a long time to come, Bill was destined to remember the awful anxiety and pleading in it. Then, at last, more sounds came, and Brent bent lower to catch them.

"…I…didn't…kill…him…" The words came in the faintest whisper, and Brent, scarcely knowing what he was doing, nodded his head with some vague idea of thereby assuring the dying man that he understood.

Strange tried again, and this time he was so successful that all five men heard him distinctly.

"I…swear…I…didn't kill…him… I…found…found… him…here… I…swear… I…" and suddenly the head rolled over onto its side. The lips worked convulsively again, and a stream of blood gushed from them. One quiver of the entire body, a faint rattling in the throat, and the man lay quite still. Henderson laid his hand over the heart, kept it there for a few moments, then rose slowly to his feet.

"That's over," he said quietly. He took a handkerchief from his pocket, unfolded it, and spread it carefully over the dead face. "We'd better leave him where he is until he can be taken away," he said heavily, and turned towards the door. The others followed him in silence, and Brent, who brought up the rear, locked the door.

Chapter Four

Five to Six (Continued)

IN THE HALL THE FIVE MEN PAUSED OUTSIDE THE STUDY door and looked at each other. In the mind of each was the same question: "What is to be done next?" and to each the same answer to the question had occurred—the police.

It was Brent who voiced their thoughts.

"Somebody'll have to go for the police," he announced gruffly and, with the exception of the old doctor, the others nodded their heads. He shook his head and patted the speaker on the back.

"It is twelve miles to Maylings," he said, and left it at that.

"I agree with Bill," boomed Sir Anthony. "Can't stay here with two bodies in the house without doing something about it. Damn nonsense, eh?"

Again the doctor shrugged his shoulders.

"By all means then, try," he said softly. "If they get here, I doubt if much can be done until this storm lifts."

"We'd better have a shot at it, anyhow," said Brent. He looked at Teddy and Tony in turn, and was about to invite the latter to accompany him, when he remembered Helen, and spoke, instead, to the former. "You come with me, Teddy. We'll take the two-seater if Tony doesn't mind."

Tony nodded with a sigh of relief, and the doctor led the way to the door leading to the kitchen, saying as he did so: "You'd better go out this way; the garage is just opposite the scullery at the back."

The other four followed him through the big kitchen into the scullery beyond, and saw him start with surprise as he came to the door of the latter.

"Has anybody been through here? Any of you, I mean?"

The others shook their heads.

"The door's unbolted," explained the doctor. "Somebody's been through it, unless they forgot to lock it last night."

He pulled it open, and Brent, followed by Teddy, passed through, running the few steps across the yard to the doors of the garage. The three men in the house watched them pull back the big doors and disappear inside.

"That's funny," remarked the doctor. "Looks as if the garage doors weren't locked, too."

They waited to see Brent and Fraser start out in the car. But this never happened. Instead, in less than three minutes the two came running out of the garage and back into the scullery.

"Somebody's been monkeying about with the cars," announced Brent. "Tyres all slashed to hell, and the valves taken out and thrown away."

"Eh? What's that?"

"Somebody's cut the tyres of all the cars," explained Brent for the second time, "and the valves are gone, so that even if we managed to patch up the tyres, we couldn't fill them."

"The petrol's all run out of the tank of the two-seater, too," added Tony.

"And they've probably done the same with the Austin Seven and the other two cars," completed Brent. "So that's that, unless we can walk it."

"Walk twelve miles in this?" The old doctor bolted the scullery doors as he spoke, and presently the five men turned back through the kitchen to the hall.

"You'd better run upstairs and get into something dry, you and Tony," said the doctor, as they crossed the hall, and Brent, remembering suddenly that he was soaked to the skin, began to shiver.

"You'd better all get to bed," Henderson continued. "There's nothing that you can do."

A low rumble of thunder made itself heard as he finished speaking, and all five stood in silence until it mounted to a cracking roar and then died away.

"We can't walk twelve miles in this, certainly," agreed Brent as he turned to the stairs.

Kay and her mother appeared at the top and came slowly down, and he stood on one side to allow them to pass, his eyes on Kay's face as she descended. She passed him without a glance and spoke to the doctor.

"Helen's asleep," she said, and the doctor nodded.

"That's good," he said. "She'll probably sleep on now for some hours, and the longer she sleeps the better. You'd better get back to bed yourself, and you, too, Lady Fane."

"But, Hendy…my dear…what about the murder?" Lady Fane cast a fearful glance in the direction of the study door, and edged nearer to her husband who put an arm about her shoulders.

"Better go up to bed, m'dear," growled Sir Anthony. "There's nothing for any of us to do down here, and you'll only tire yourself out." He propelled her gently towards the stairs, and she went unresistingly. "And you, too, Kay," Sir Anthony continued. "Come along."

But Kay did not move. She seemed to be suddenly deep in thought, and her father frowned as he spoke to her again.

"Hear me, Kay? Upstairs, my girl."

Kay came out of her sudden reverie and raised her head up. She looked at each of them in turn, with the exception of Brent, who was watching her closely. Her reply made him start with surprise.

"I think I'll stay down here, if you don't mind," she said. "Come and keep me company, Teddy." She turned to Fraser and linked her arm in his. "We'll go and resume our talk in the drawing-room," she continued. "And nobody need be either afraid or shocked." She gave just one fleeting glance at Brent's face before she went on in a dry, cold little voice. "Teddy and I are going to be married," she said. "It's a funny moment to choose for such an announcement, but perhaps it will make your minds easier on our account, and help to persuade you that we are not misbehaving ourselves. Come along, Teddy."

And with that Kay pulled Teddy in the direction of the drawing-room. The others watched them disappear through the door, and as it closed behind them Lady Fane commenced to cry weakly.

"Well, I'm damned!" remarked Sir Anthony with his voice at full strength again. "I will be damned, sir! What with murders and sudden deaths and illness and engagements...what's going to happen next, I should like to know?" And bestowing a glare upon the hall in general, he pushed his weeping, unre-sisting wife before him up the stairs and stamped up after her.

Tony made his way past Brent and followed his parents, and presently Brent became aware that Henderson was pat-ting him gently on the shoulder.

"Go and get into bed, Bill," said the doctor kindly. "I'll bring you up a drink."

Brent pulled himself together, and with a muttered word of thanks, he, too, went slowly up the stairs and along the corridor at the top to his own room. Once inside he stripped himself of his wet clothes, indulged in a vigorous towelling, and tumbled into bed.

So Kay had read his unspoken thoughts?

He lay on his back and stared at the ceiling. In the morning he must, of course, apologise fully to her, and then he must commence the task of forgetting all about her, and there was only one way that he knew of in which this could be done. He must resign his job and go away. He would go on the fol-lowing day. The following day? It was morning already. What he meant was later in the day, as soon as the police came...

The thought of the police brought his thoughts back from Kay's sudden announcement and concentrated them on the room beneath, where two bodies lay. There would, of course, be an inquest, and without doubt, he would have to give evidence. Then, with something of a shock, he remembered suddenly the discovery of the little clock on the floor in the study, and his discussion with the doctor. Manning had been deliberately and foully murdered. Strange, on the very point of death, had sworn it had not been he who had committed the crime, and if Strange was to be believed, then who was the murderer?

As the question occurred to him, Brent sat up in bed with something of a jerk, for the answer to the question followed, in his mind, immediately upon the question itself.

Somebody in the house had murdered Manning, unless, of course, some stranger had made his way into the study, out of the storm.

Brent almost sighed with relief as the idea came to him, but even as he did so, he began to doubt it. The murderer from outside must have entered the house through the study windows, and if Manning was there at the time, and awake, would there not have been a struggle which he, himself, would have heard?

Twenty to two was the time at which the clock had stopped, and at twenty to two he, himself, had been wide awake. Kay and Fraser had been downstairs in the drawing-room, and surely they, too, would have heard. Tony, also, had said that he had been awake, and that provided another set of ears to hear. Surely Manning would have called out!

No, the idea of the stranger was an improbable one. Somebody inside the house had murdered Manning— somebody who had gone to him in his study, and was able to do so without causing any noisy outbreak from him. But who in the house would commit such a crime, and why?

Without realising the full import of what he was doing, Brent commenced to go over in his mind the occupants of the house.

First, Mrs. Geraint, whom he had seen emerging from the dining-room and going upstairs, walking in her sleep. She might have done it. Hadn't she been upset because of her cat and kittens? Would such a thing be enough to drive her to murder in her sleep?

Then Kay and Fraser. What had they been doing downstairs all that time from one o'clock? Brent's mind went back to the scene in the laboratory when the kitten had died so horribly, and he recalled the hatred and anger Kay had displayed. But the idea was ridiculous—utterly absurd. To hate a man is one thing; to murder him is something remote from it. Still, they were downstairs, and hadn't Fraser said something in the laboratory about Manning being killed—something to the effect that Manning ought to be killed for what he had done to the kitten?

Henderson? But Henderson had come with him to find the body. What had he been doing since he had gone to bed? And what earthly motive had such a man as Henderson for such a crime?

Then there was Helen, and here Brent's heart gave a leap, for his mind was filling with the memory of Helen's delirium, of the broken words of hatred and fear that she had uttered as she lay unconscious on the couch; a delirium in which she seemed to be going over some dreadful scene in which she and her father had played the only two parts. Could it be possible that Helen, in a sudden fit of fear and hatred, had struck her father down? She had been awake just after he, Brent, had discovered the tragedy; she had, in fact, crept upon them unawares. How long had she been awake? Where had she come from to the study? How long before had that scene which she had gone over in her delirium happened?

Who else was there? Sir Anthony and Lady Fane. The latter Brent dismissed immediately from his mind. Sir Anthony, who had appeared, fully dressed, as he, Brent, had carried Helen across the hall from the study door; where had he come from? That, of course, could easily be ascertained, for there would be the evidence of Lady Fane to go upon.

Remained only Tony, and what had he said about himself? Ah, yes! That he had been in his room the whole time, sitting up in a chair, until he had found Strange walking about in the corridor.

Mrs. Geraint, Kay, Fraser, Henderson, Sir Anthony, Lady Fane, and Tony. Strike out Sir Anthony and his wife, who were together in their own room, and could speak for each other... The other servants, of course. One of them might just as easily have done it. Their movements could be ascertained quite easily in the morning, and if one of them was missing, there would be a definite indication. How many were there? He recalled that, as far as he knew, there were only two, both of whom he had seen the night before about the house. Both were girls, and quite young; and they probably shared a room between them.

Anybody else? Why, of course... He leaned back on his pillows and smiled grimly. He had forgotten himself. He, like the others, had nobody to speak for him. He had spent the time right up to four o'clock asleep in his room; he had been the first on the scene of the crime, but hadn't he read somewhere of a story in which the murderer was heard calling for help, and discovered by the body of his victim, putting up a magnificent show of having come upon the corpse, and having immediately given the alarm?

Could it have been Strange, after all? What, in any case, had the butler been doing in the study? Attempting to steal something from the safe—something which he must have wanted very badly to make him stay there with a murdered man in order to find it. But again Brent remembered the terrible agony of anxiety in the man's one remaining eye as he looked up at him. No, if ever a man spoke the truth, that man was Strange as he lay dying.

Came a knock at the door, and Henderson entered, bringing with him the promised drink—a stiff whisky and soda. Brent took the glass and drank its contents gratefully, while the doctor seated himself on the bed and watched him.

"What you might call a night of excitement, Hendy," said Brent, stretching out his hand and putting the glass down on the small table at the side of his bed.

The doctor nodded moodily.

"Yes...yes," he replied. "What you might certainly call a full night. And the storm," he added, "is as bad as ever."

There fell a silence between them until, at last, Brent raised himself on one elbow and looked at the doctor.

"Look here, Hendy," he said. "What other servants are there in the house besides Mrs. Geraint, and—well, Strange is dead now."

"Two girls," replied the doctor. "Why?"

"Because," returned Brent, "I don't believe Strange killed Manning, and that means that one of the rest of us did."

Henderson nodded thoughtfully.

"If you cut out Strange," he said, "I suppose you're right; I expect the police will soon find out what happened. It takes the trained mind to do so." He got to his feet.

"And, by the way, Hendy," continued Brent, "have you any idea what it was that Strange was trying to steal from that safe?"

Henderson shrugged his shoulders.

"Money, I suppose?" hinted Brent.

"Shouldn't think so. Manning never kept a lot of money in the house. I've been thinking over precisely the same thing, and the only thing I can imagine Strange wanting to steal as badly as all that is the formula for Manning's new gas. That would be valuable in the hands of a traitor—if Strange was one."

"To sell to another government, eh?"

Henderson nodded, and stepped towards the door.

"But, as I said," he remarked as he reached it, "the police will soon find all that out. I'm going to have a look at Helen."

"What is going to happen there? Anything serious?"

"I don't know for certain. You never can tell in these cases of shocks. It depends upon so many things." Henderson paused with his hand on the door, his eyes bent to the ground before him. "I'm hoping," he continued presently, "that Helen will come out of it without harm. On the other hand, she might— well—, one can never tell." He looked up and gave Brent one of his quiet smiles. "I should get some sleep if I were you, old man." He turned to go, then once again he paused and looked up at Brent. "By the way, Bill," he said, "I shouldn't worry too much about Kay's announcement tonight if I were you."

Brent reddened suddenly, and the doctor smiled as he saw it.

"I know Kay very well," he continued, "much better than most other people, yourself included, and I don't think she was terribly serious. Cheero!"

Another swift smile, and the doctor had gone. Brent lay back in his bed thinking of what his visitor had said, and it was just at that moment that Teddy Fraser, seated by the side of Kay in the drawing-room beneath, turned to her and broke a silence that had lasted ever since they had entered.

"I say, Kay, old thing," he said, "you didn't really mean what you said just now in the hall, did you?"

Kay turned a pair of troubled blue eyes upon him, and slowly shook her head.

"No, Teddy," she replied, "I didn't."

Teddy leaned forward, placed his elbows on his knees and cupped his face in his hands.

"I thought not," he said miserably.

Kay sighed at the misery in his voice, and presently and without warning, she commenced to cry quietly.

"I say, old thing," said Teddy, putting his arm about her. "You mustn't, you know; you really mustn't."

Kay continued to cry on his shoulder for some minutes, and he let her do so undisturbed, thereby establishing a claim to the understanding of women. Presently, she started up and stood away from him.

"You oughtn't to love me, Teddy dear," she said wildly.

"Bu-but I can't help it, old thing."

"But you must help it. I'm not worth it. In fact I'm the worst woman alive. I'm something worse than that, too," she went on, the tears running unrestrained down her face, "I'm a fool! I'm the biggest fool in a skirt that was ever seen on this world. A bad lot and a fool! There! Now you know what you've escaped."

And without another word Kay turned and ran from the room, leaving Mr. Fraser upon his feet, staring after her in amazement.

A moment later and he, too, made his way up the stairs and to his room.

Chapter Five

Six to Seven

Six o'clock was normally the hour at which the first sign of life would make its appearance about Treeholme in the shape of a man from a neighbouring farm who, approaching the house by way of the front drive, would walk around it to the back, deposit three pints of fresh milk upon the kitchen doorstep, and then depart the way he had come. Thereupon the quiet of repose would once more descend upon the place until half-past six, when it would be banished for the day by the vigorous opening of the kitchen and scullery windows by Alice and her colleague Mary, the two maids.

The opening of the windows would be followed by the unbolting and opening of the kitchen door, and this latter, in its turn, by the disappearance of the milk, some of which would, in the course of some ten minutes, end its short experience—if milk can be said to possess experience—of this planet in the cup of tea with which Mrs. Geraint was wont to stay herself in preparation for the coming day.

But this morning proved an exception to the general rule.

To begin with no man appeared with the milk, for the storm was still in possession, and was successfully defying all and sundry to venture out in it. It seemed to be working around the district in a circle, for the thunder came and went, now seeming to be right overhead, now far away. The rain filled the air and beat down with merciless persistency upon the earth beneath. It collected in the neighbouring fields; it poured down the side of the roof of Treeholme and cascaded over the edges in an unfailing stream; it ran down the gravel drive in rivulets which became ever broader and deeper; not very far away from the bottom of the garden it was busy turning a peaceful stream into a turbulent flood; and ever and anon came the lightning to make it shine, for one brilliant second, in field, river, and air with ten million scintillations.

Few things could live in that rain. It beat the grass flat; it caught the frightened bird which ventured from its shelter, and beat that, too, until it dropped dead upon the ground; and then it beat upon the little body, pushing it hither and thither, and finally pushing it into some stream or rivulet of its own making where it covered it up altogether and washed it away out of sight.

On the night before, it had kept both Alice and Mary awake so that they might shiver with fright at the thunder and the lightning, and duck their heads beneath the bedclothes whenever these came to fill the air with terrific sound and light. And this, perhaps, is why half-past six came and went, and not even an attempt was made to open a window; for at last, being both young and healthy, the two girls had fallen asleep out of sheer exhaustion, and were still fast asleep.

For the rest, the house was still, within. The doctor was

quiet and silent as he sat at the bedside of the sleeping Helen, one of her hands held lightly in his own. Sir Anthony and Lady Fane were quiet, both of them having dozed off to sleep. Brent was quiet, lying on his back in order that his view of the blank ceiling might enable him to go over and over again the events of the night before. Tony was quiet, for that was the condition upon which the doctor allowed him to sit at the other side of Helen's bed. Young Mr. Fraser sat in a chair in his room, so quiet that he might have been carved out of wood. He was brooding upon the hopelessness of life, and wondering if loneliness was better to be borne in the depths of some foreign jungle. Kay was both silent and invisible, for she had covered her head with the bedclothes, beneath which she was crying so quietly that no one could have suspected her presence there, had he been compelled to rely only upon his sense of hearing. Mrs. Geraint was almost quiet—not quite because of a certain stertorousness in her breathing, and an occasional uneasy movement of her body; but even she was, on the whole, marvellously still, considering the noise of the rain, the cut on her right hand, and the blood upon her nightdress.

And down in the study were the two quietest of them all; for these two had become still with the complete stillness of death, and no sound came from them, no movement, no idea, even, of life. Even the thunder which, now and then, burst with deafening cannonade above the house and round about it, left them cold and as still as ever.

Chapter Six

Seven to Eight

MRS. GERAINT AWOKE AT SEVEN OUT OF A TROUBLED dream in which she, armed with a large carving knife, was threatening the oncoming figure of her master. There, before her, was the tight-lipped, sneering face with its half-closed eyes. In each hand was held a wriggling kitten from which blood dripped. Nearer and nearer came the figure until it was bending right over her and the blood dripped down upon her nightdress. With one last despairing effort, she drew back the knife to strike, thrust it forward with all her might, uttered a stifled shriek, and awoke.

She sat up in bed trembling and perspiring, the terror of her dream still upon her. Her hand was clenched before her on the eiderdown. She opened it slowly, and gazed at it with fresh terror, for across the top of the palm was a shallow cut, and the blood from it covered her hand.

She pushed back the bedclothes and gasped as she saw a large stain upon her nightdress, and she was about to jump out of bed and scream for help, when she suddenly remembered that she was awake. The clock upon her mantelpiece helped her by striking seven, and instead of jumping out and giving reins to her terror, she switched on the light above her bed and calmed down.

One of her bad nights again. The first she had had for some months now; the first, in fact, since that dreadful night when she had awakened in the corridor outside Mr. Manning's room to find his face not a foot away from her own.

But where did this blood upon her hand and nightdress come from? Had she been sleep-walking again, and somehow managed to cut her hand without it waking her? She must have done so; else, how to explain this blood. She had dreamed of a knife. Perhaps she had played with one in her sleep.

She shuddered and snuggled down again in the bed, drawing the sheets tight about her shoulders. Soon now Alice would come with her morning tea, and while she waited, she would rest a little more and calm herself.

As she did so, she allowed her thoughts to go back to the night before. She remembered that she had not been very well. The matter of the kittens had upset her, and, of course, she had fainted. Perhaps she had cut herself during the faint, and failed to notice it when they had put her to bed. She recalled that she had felt very drowsy and heavy about the head.

It was the taking of the kittens and the cat that had upset her so much. She thought of them now, and wondered what Manning had done with them; and as she thought about it, she came to a decision towards which she had been travelling for some time since. She would leave Treeholme and its hateful master. Miss Helen would soon be married. She would ask her to take her—Mrs. Geraint—into her new house, and until then she would go away to Sarah's for a rest. No doubt Mr. Tony would be seeing Miss Helen every day, and the girl would no longer be left alone with that monster of a father.

Yes, she would tell Mr. Manning that she was leaving, and go as soon as she could—tomorrow, if possible.

Having made the decision, Mrs. Geraint felt calmer, and began to look forward to her cup of tea. Alice was late this morning. What had become of the girl? The storm, perhaps, keeping her awake through the night, and causing her to oversleep herself. Well, she'd give the girl another ten minutes, and if nothing happened at the end of that time, she, Mrs. Geraint, would get up herself and go and find out what had become of the maids.

The ten minutes came and passed, and still no Alice. Well, she would give the girl another five. That would make it quarter-past seven. After all, the night had been a very bad one. In fact, the storm was still raging, and no doubt everybody would feel the better for a little extra sleep.

But before the five minutes were up, Mrs. Geraint had dropped off into a light doze herself, and five minutes later she was fast asleep.

Asleep? No, wide awake, intent upon getting out of bed as she had said she would.

Carefully she pushed the bedclothes back and lifted her feet over the side. Then she raised herself upright without noise and stood listening. Somewhere out there in the corridor was that sneering, horrible face waiting for her, and sooner or later she must meet it. She wanted to meet it. She was tired of being afraid of it. Until she met it face to face, and struck it down, she would never know peace again. There were the kittens, too, to be saved. When she had dealt with the face she would search for the kittens and take them away with her. Now, what should she take to fight the face with? The knife! Where had she left the knife? Ah! she remembered. It was down on the dining-room table where she, herself, had put it. She would go out to the face, drive it before her until she could get the knife, and then...

Very quietly, and with infinite care, she crept to the door and peeped out. No sign of the face. It was downstairs, perhaps, waiting for her.

She made her way noiselessly along the corridor until she arrived at the end. There she paused, for she thought she heard a sound behind her—the sound of a door opening. She turned, but saw nothing.

Down the stairs went Mrs. Geraint, and after her, with cat-like tread, crept Brent, pausing when she paused, doing his best to step in time with her.

At last she reached the hall below. Still no sign of the face. All the better. She would now be able to get the knife undisturbed. She went into the dining-room and up to the big table. Here she paused, a troubled frown appearing between her eyes. There was no knife here. It had gone. The face, perhaps, had taken it. She must find it. She must get that knife somehow.

Brent, waiting outside at the foot of the stairs, saw her come through the dining-room door and turn down the hall. With a start of surprise he watched her make unerringly for the study door and stepped forward to prevent her opening it, when suddenly it occurred to him that here, perhaps, in this further sleep-walking of Mrs. Geraint, he might find the key to the mystery of the killing of Horace Manning. He stood, therefore, and watched her while she fumbled with the key in the door, heard the click as she turned it, and, making no noise with his bare feet, he crept up behind her.

But, careful as he had been, she paused, threw her head up, and a second later, had turned to face him. His heart stood still as he saw the blood upon her hand and nightdress, and he stood as if turned to stone while her unseeing eyes stared right through him.

Then, presently, after what seemed an age to him, she turned again to the door, turned the knob, and pushed it open.

Brent watched with bated breath. A moment's pause on the threshold, and the white-clad figure crept noiselessly across it, and paused again inside, her head moving slowly from side to side, unintelligible mutterings coming from her mouth.

Then a bloodstained hand went out before her, and she walked slowly forward. Brent stifled a gasp as he saw the direction in which the hand was going. Another foot, and it would touch the knife. Nearer and nearer went the hand. Another two inches…an inch… Brent felt his heart leap within him as he saw the outstretched hand touch the white ivory handle, saw the fingers curl about it and tighten into a grasp.

Then suddenly the figure before him stiffened, the head jerked upwards, and scream after scream came from it.

Brent leaped forward in time to catch it as it fell backwards, the last scream dying in her throat, a strangled gurgle, and as he fell beneath the dead weight, he heard the sounds of footsteps hurrying down the stairs and across the hall.

Chapter Seven

Eight to Nine

"Oh, my Gawd! She's gone and done it as she said she would. Oh, my goodness to gracious me! Oh…oh…!"

Alice cannoned up against Brent as he rose slowly and painfully from beneath the considerable bulk of the unconscious Mrs. Geraint. Mary, the other maid, was staring, pale-faced, through the open door of the study.

"Good God, sir!" boomed the voice of Sir Anthony from the stairs, and at the sound of it, Alice renewed her screams.

"She said she would kill him, and she's done it! Oh, my Gawd, we shall all be murdered, we shall…"

The girl's voice cracked into the laughter of hysterics, and Brent, seizing her by the elbows, ran her across the hall and pushed her through the door which led to the kitchen. Returning to the recumbent form of the housekeeper, over which Sir Anthony, Teddy, and Kay were now standing, he ordered the second maid to follow her colleague, whose screams still reached them from behind the kitchen door.

He spoke to her twice without effect, and laid a hand on her shoulder.

"Mary," he said sharply, "d'you hear what I say? Go and look after Alice; we'll attend to Mrs. Geraint."

The girl turned her chalk-white face upon him, and Brent was appalled at the terror in it.

"Alice was right," she whispered. "Mrs. Geraint said she would kill the master…"

"Never mind that now," said Brent soothingly. "Go and look after Alice."

"She said she would do it with the knife. She said so last night. She said…"

Brent interrupted her again, taking her firmly by the arm and leading her towards the back of the hall.

"We'll go into all that presently," he said. "You go and look after Alice, and make us a cup of tea."

The mention of one of her ordinary duties seemed to have a good effect, for the girl, who had seemed almost paralysed with fright and shock, pulled herself together, and Brent watched her disappear through the kitchen door with a sigh of relief.

Anthony and Kay had joined the little group at the other end of the hall, and Lady Fane, who was on her way down the stairs, called out to him:

"Bill…my dear… What has happened? All that screaming… Has somebody else been killed? My dear…"

"There you are, you see?" boomed Sir Anthony. "Housekeeper killed him in her sleep, eh? Dreadful affair! Terrible! Question is, what's to be done now, eh?"

"Get her upstairs to bed," replied Brent as he rejoined them. "Come on, lend me a hand."

Teddy and Tony attached themselves to the unconscious woman's feet while Brent took her head and shoulders, and with much heaving and pushing and pulling, the three of them managed to carry the dead weight up the stairs and along the corridor at the top to Mrs. Geraint's room, where they laid her on the bed with gasps of relief, and stood on one side while the doctor, who had come from Helen's room, examined her.

"Nothing more than a bad faint," he said presently. "Shock, and no doubt a little trouble when she wakes, but she'll be all right in a day or so. One of the maids can look after her. I'm going back to Helen."

And having rung for Mary and given her instructions, all four men left the room, the doctor to return to his vigil at Helen's bedside; the other three to go downstairs again to discuss the most recent of the sensational happenings which had come to make life so strange and complicated an affair for them all.

Lady Fane had been conducted in a half-fainting condition into the drawing-room by her daughter and husband, and there the three men found her being comforted and soothed.

"She won't go to bed," bellowed Sir Anthony as they entered the room.

"Do shut up, Father." Kay's voice was exasperated. "We aren't deaf, and there has been quite enough row already this morning. What with you, and Mrs. Geraint, and the maids and the thunder! It's enough to drive anybody mad."

"Mad?" Sir Anthony puffed his cheeks. "Mad, did you say? Huh! Two murders and one death in one night…"

"She's not dead," said Brent wearily. "She only fainted."

"But, Bill…my dear…" Lady Fane commenced to cry weakly.

"Look here," said Brent firmly. "What it all means I don't know any more than any of you do. I saw Mrs. Geraint walking in her sleep, and I followed her. She went to the study, unlocked the door…"

"In her sleep?" Sir Anthony was incredulous, and sounded it.

"In her sleep," repeated Brent.

"What sane woman would go to that room awake?" demanded Kay.

"And she collapsed inside the door," continued Brent. "She must have awakened suddenly and seen the…the…"

"The bodies," finished Teddy helpfully, and Lady Fane, at the last word, wailed aloud.

"And what about the blood on her nightdress?" demanded Sir Anthony.

"She'd cut her hand," replied Brent.

"When?" Sir Anthony put the question in the manner of a counsel bullying a witness into a damaging admission. "The blood on her hand was dry. Question is, when did the woman cut her hand, eh?"

"How do I know?" Brent's head was beginning to ache again.

"That reminds me," said Teddy, and everybody looked at him. "We saw Mrs. Geraint walking about with a knife in her hand, didn't we, Kay?"

"When was that?" It was Brent who asked the question.

"When we were down here before…when we went into the drawing-room."

"I saw her first," Kay interrupted him. "That was why I came downstairs in the first place." She flung a defiant glance at Brent. "I was awake and heard somebody outside my door. I got up to see who it was, and when I saw it was Mrs. Geraint walking in her sleep, I followed her down and met Teddy, here."

"Well? What about the knife?"

"She was carrying it in her right hand," Teddy continued the story, "like a dagger…"

"Like a what?" bellowed Sir Anthony.

"Like a dagger. Like this." Teddy took a pencil from his pocket and demonstrated.

"Good God!" ejaculated Sir Anthony.

"What did she do with it?" asked Brent.

"Took it into the dining-room and put it on the table."

"What?"

"She took it into the dining-room and put it on the table." Sir Anthony snorted.

"Why?"

"Couldn't say, sir." Teddy's voice was apologetic.

"Was there any blood on her nightdress then?" Brent wanted to know.

Teddy shook his head.

"Don't remember any, do you, Kay?"

Kay shook her head too.

"Well, what happened then?"

"She went upstairs to bed. At least"—Teddy corrected himself—"she went upstairs."

"And we," Kay cut in with a toss of her head, "went and misconducted ourselves on the settee in the drawing-room."

"Kay…my dear…" Lady Fane raised a tear-stained face.

"Well," retorted Kay, "that's what you all thought, wasn't it? In any case we went and slept together. Put it like that, if you like."

"And you told me, Bill," Sir Anthony turned to Brent, "that

you saw her again coming out of the dining-room when you came down."

"Let's get this straight." Brent found and lit a cigarette, and the others waited for him to resume. "What time was it, Kay, when you came down?"

"Just after one o'clock." Kay's voice was still defiant, and she did not look at him as she answered. Brent put his next question to Teddy.

"Did you hear her come down again after she had gone upstairs?"

Teddy shook his head.

"How long after you came in here with Kay did you stay awake?" continued Brent, and then, as Teddy coloured, he went on: "I'm only trying to work the thing out; I'm not—er—"

"About twenty minutes," said Kay shortly. "Teddy always takes about twenty minutes to propose, and as soon as he had done so, I fell asleep. At least," she continued, "I must have done so, because that was the last thing I remembered."

"So that," Brent went on, still concentrating on Teddy, "for all you know, Mrs. Geraint might have been walking about for some time?"

"As far as I know," agreed Teddy.

"Did she have blood on her when you saw her, Bill?" This was Sir Anthony's question.

Brent shrugged his shoulders.

"That's just what I'm trying to remember," he said. "Perhaps Hendy will remember. He saw her more closely than I did."

There followed a moment of silence which was broken, eventually, by one of Sir Anthony's eloquent snorts.

"Plain as a pikestaff," he barked. "Woman said last night

she'd kill him. Girl said so just now. Woman went to bed, dreamed it, got it on her mind, walked in her sleep, came downstairs, found the knife, and killed him."

"And he just sat there and let her do it?" Kay turned a withering glance on her father, which drew another snort from that gentleman.

"Might have been asleep himself," he boomed. "Dammit! Quite possible, eh?"

They all considered the possibility in silence, but Sir Anthony who glowered at them in turn saw nothing but doubt on their faces, and had it been somebody else who had made the suggestion, he would have been the first to scout the idea of such a man as Manning falling asleep in his study, and allowing himself to be murdered without even waking up.

"It is possible, of course," agreed Brent, tactfully. "But… but…" He tailed off into doubtful silence, and Sir Anthony, determined to see it through, wheeled round on him.

"But what? Come on, out with it! Why shouldn't she have killed him?"

"Well! Is it likely, sir, that a woman walking in her sleep would kill a man like that with one blow? So that he died without making a sound, almost?"

"How d'you know he didn't make a sound?"

Brent got up and paced the room.

"I was awake in the room above," he said. "Kay and Teddy were in here, and probably awake too. Tony was awake. I'm sure I would have heard something. He must have died instantaneously and almost without a sound, and it doesn't seem likely to me that a woman striking in her sleep like that would have struck so surely."

"Of course not!" Kay lit a cigarette and blew a mouthful of smoke into the air with disdainful emphasis. "Even if she'd been awake, she probably wouldn't have been able to do it with one blow. And in any case"—she turned to her father— "Mrs. Geraint wasn't the only one who said she'd like to kill him. I said so, and I jolly well meant it, too."

"Kay…my dear…" Her mother turned a despairing face upon her daughter.

Kay tossed her head.

"What's the good of pretending?" she said. "Which of us here wouldn't have killed him last night in the laboratory? If I'd had a knife or some of his beastly gas, I most certainly would have done so. And so would you, too; and you—and you." She looked from her father to Brent, and to Teddy. "Why," she went on, "Teddy here was so worked up about the kittens that he came down to break into the lab. to get them out. That's how we met; wasn't it, Teddy?"

Teddy thus appealed to looked up, and coloured again as he found the others looking at him. Brent raised his eyebrows at this item of information.

"What time did you get down here, Teddy?" he asked.

"I don't know." Teddy pulled at his chin and looked more embarrassed than ever. "I suppose I must have been down about half an hour before Kay came."

"And what were you doing all that time?"

"Trying to get into the laboratory," he replied.

Sir Anthony took up the questioning.

"What d'you mean—trying to get into the laboratory? Through the window?"

"No, sir. The door."

"Through the door?" Sir Anthony had put on his bullying counsel manner again.

"He couldn't very well get in through the wall, could he?" asked Kay with heavy sarcasm, and ignoring the glare with which it was received by her parent.

"I was trying to pick the lock," replied Teddy.

"To get the cats out, eh?"

"Yes, sir."

"And you didn't succeed, eh?"

"No, sir."

"And you were down here for half an hour by yourself?" This question came from Brent.

Teddy nodded his head, and Brent followed it up with another.

"And you saw nobody during that time?"

"No."

"And heard nothing from the study?"

"Nothing at all."

Another silence fell upon them, a silence during which Teddy became more and more embarrassed.

"I say," he said presently, his face a bright red which faded slowly as he spoke, "you aren't suggesting that I killed him, are you?"

Nobody answered, and he started to his feet.

"Look here, Bill," he continued, "what are you getting at?"

"If it comes to that," interrupted Kay, "what were you doing at that time?" She was looking straight at Brent, who received her question with amazement.

"I?"

"Why not? What were you doing, anyhow?"

"I was in my room."

"And did anybody see you there?"

Brent stared around him, his amazement growing. Suddenly he laughed out loud.

"I'm not suggesting that anybody killed Manning," he said presently.

"I should hope not!" barked Sir Anthony, and would have said more, but Kay proceeded to take the wind out of his sails.

"And what about you, Father?" she asked sweetly. "What were you doing?"

"What the devil…" began Sir Anthony, and then paused, his face the picture of astonishment. "I went to the bathroom at about half-past one," he said, "and stayed there for some little time. Your mother here was sleeping on the bed…"

"So she couldn't corroborate your statement, eh?" Kay did not wait for her answer. She turned to her brother.

"What about you, Tony?"

"Don't talk damn nonsense, Kay," was all the answer she got.

"And there was Helen too," continued Kay. "I don't know what happened to her after I came down. And couldn't mother have slipped out of her room and back again while father was gone?"

This last suggestion brought a horrified gasp from Lady Fane. Kay threw the end of her cigarette into an ash-tray and yawned.

"There it is," she said. "Nobody to verify any of us. Even Teddy might have slipped away while I was asleep, and come back again. And so, too, could I. There was the knife waiting on the dining-room table for anybody to pick up, and somebody did pick it up."

"This," announced Sir Anthony, bringing his hand down heavily on his knee, "is a lot of damn fiddle-de-dee. It's as plain as a pikestaff. Mrs. Geraint did it, and…"

A low rumble of thunder interrupted him. In the middle of it there came the sound of running feet outside the door, and they all turned towards it as it burst open to reveal Mary who ran a few steps into the room and stood there panting with agitation.

"It's Mrs. Geraint," she gasped. "I can't do nothing with her. She's come to and she's afraid they're going to take and have her hung for killing master, and I don't know what to do with her, and please will somebody come at once."

And having delivered this message between gasps, the girl turned and bolted out of the room and up the stairs.

"There you are, eh?" said Sir Anthony triumphantly. "She's confessed."

He strode to the door, followed by Brent, Teddy, and Tony.

Chapter Eight

Eight to Nine (Continued)

THEY FOUND THE HOUSEKEEPER SITTING UP IN BED, weeping hysterically, and in a state bordering upon collapse.

Sir Anthony took up a position at the foot of the bed, cleared his throat, and glared down at the unfortunate woman.

"Now, my good woman," he boomed. "Tell us all about it. Why did you kill your master? Come on, now."

Brent made a gesture of despair at this opening which had the natural effect of throwing Mrs. Geraint into more paroxysms of weeping and moaning, in the middle of which she managed to gasp out something to the effect that she did not mean to do it. He sent Anthony for the doctor, and presently Henderson entered the room in time to interrupt another question from Sir Anthony which would have rendered the possibility of any sort of cohesion on Mrs. Geraint's part more remote than ever.

Taking charge of the situation, and silencing Sir Anthony with a quietly spoken word of warning, Henderson sat down by the side of the bed. Not until he had arranged the pillows, made the nearly hysterical woman lie back on them, and sent Mary hurrying off to prepare a "nice, strong cup of tea," did he bother her with words, and they were words of comfort and reassurance which he spoke to her.

She grew gradually calmer, and presently the doctor stepped away from the bed and motioned to the others to leave the room.

"You have a good long rest, Mrs. Geraint," he advised her, "and when you are better we'll all have a talk about it."

But the worthy housekeeper was determined to get it over and done with, and she struggled up into a sitting position amongst her pillows.

"I'll never rest again, sir," she assured them, "until I've spoken, and you've got to listen to me."

"Quite right too," boomed Sir Anthony. "The woman wants to confess. She'll feel easier in her mind afterwards."

Mrs. Geraint nodded, as if to herself.

"I never meant to do it, sir, that I'll swear to on the Bible," she said, her voice quivering with her recent weeping. "I didn't know I was doing it, as you might say, sir. I just woke up, and there was my hand on the knife and him d-d-dead." She shuddered violently, and the doctor laid a restraining hand upon her shoulder. But she seemed determined to go on with it, and controlled herself with an obvious effort. "I knew I would do it sooner or later," she continued. "He always hated Miss Helen, and he hated me for loving her. He used to frighten her at nights by just standing over her cot till she woke and screamed and woke me too, and I would find him just standing over her cot looking down at the child. He was evil…evil… He used to gloat over her terror, and when I had words with him, he would just look at me with those eyes and somehow or other…" She placed a hand to her throat and shuddered again. "He would find animals—cats and little dogs, and kill them in his laboratory. I only stayed for Miss Helen's sake, but I got to dreaming about him. I dreamed night after night that he was following me through the house, just his sneering, evil face in the darkness, and once…once…I woke up and found myself outside in the passage with him standing not a yard away from me, watching…watching… I fainted, and when I came to he was gone, and Miss Helen was there with me, crying as if her heart would break." Mrs. Geraint cried herself, holding her face between her hands, and rocking gently from side to side. The men waited in silence for her to continue which, presently, she did. "Then last night," she said, "I dreamed again, the same old dream. I dreamed it twice, and it was different. The kittens came into it this time. He was following me, holding them up in his hands for me to see how they suffered, and something inside me rose up at the sight of them, and I made up my mind to kill him. I…I thought in my dream I would find the knife and go and look for him. I did it, and I found his face waiting for me again in the passage outside, and I followed it downstairs to his study. Then…then I killed him there, and I woke to find the knife in his body and my hand on the knife." She paused again, studying the faces of her audience through tear-filled eyes. "I had to tell you," she went on presently. "Whatever happens to me, that's the gospel truth. I was asleep when I did it, and I couldn't have known what I was doing, could I?" She turned to the doctor at her side. "What will they do to me, Doctor?" she asked him.

Henderson patted her on the shoulder.

"You've been dreaming, Mrs. Geraint," he said kindly. "You didn't kill Mr. Manning. He had been dead for a long time before you awoke."

She stared at him with wide eyes.

"You mean that?" she asked, brokenly, and stared again as he nodded smilingly.

"You've just been dreaming," he repeated. "And now you drink that tea when Mary comes up and go to sleep again, and when you wake up I'll give you something to calm those nerves of yours. There now!"

He patted her again on the shoulder.

"But just a moment." Sir Anthony bent over the end of the bed and cleared his throat again. Henderson turned his gently smiling face towards him, and spoke quietly.

"Mrs. Geraint is going to sleep now, Sir Anthony," he said, and there was that in his quiet voice which silenced the other. "There'll be plenty of time to talk things over again."

Sir Anthony nodded and turned to the door. One by one the others followed him, Henderson, who went last, sending the now comforted housekeeper a friendly little smile before he closed the door behind him.

"So that mystery is solved," said Sir Anthony from the top of the stairs which he had reached by the time the doctor, the last to leave Mrs. Geraint's room, was outside Helen's door, half-way down the corridor. The baronet's words made him pause with his hand on the knob of this, and instead of entering Helen's room he joined the group at the head of the stairs.

"You really believe Mrs. Geraint killed Manning?" he asked in his gentle voice.

"Why not?" returned Sir Anthony.

Henderson shook his head and smiled.

"You heard what she said? The dream in which she thought she killed him happened just before she woke, and that was some hours after Manning was killed."

"And what about her previous sleep-walking? Dammit man! She's been walking most of the night. Kay and Fraser saw her just after one, and, for all we know, she was walking off and on after that. You, yourself, saw her at four."

Again Henderson shook his head.

"Sleep-walkers remember their dreams just as easily as other people," he said. "And they dream what they do in their sleep. The very shock of the impact of the knife in the body would have wakened her, to begin with, and what was he doing at the time? Allowing her to kill him without protesting?"

"The very point I made," Brent put in.

"And what about the blood on her hand and nightdress?" Sir Anthony asked.

Henderson shrugged his shoulders.

"That cut on her hand is nothing more than a deep scratch. I've examined it, and I don't believe it was made with a knife. She probably bleeds very easily." The doctor went to the door and stood there for a moment deep in thought. The others watched him in silence. "There's another and important point," he said, presently, looking up at them. "Manning died instantaneously. It takes knowledge or great luck to kill a man instantaneously with a knife, so that there is the minimum amount of bleeding and suffering. Whoever killed Manning with that knife struck with either great skill or incredible luck."

He nodded to them all and passed through the door on his way back to Helen's bedside, leaving another moody silence behind him.

Kay broke it at last with the sound of the match she struck to light another cigarette.

"Hm!" said Sir Anthony in his deep voice. "That's all very well as far as it goes, but it doesn't go very far, eh?"

There fell yet another silence, then suddenly Teddy, who had been sitting staring miserably at the carpet beneath his feet, looked up and caught Kay's troubled stare upon him.

"What is it, Kay?" he asked, and the others looked towards her.

She turned away from them and walked slowly to the windows. Teddy's face paled.

"I say," he said, starting up, "I know what you mean; my—my two years reading medicine. Look here, everybody. I—I swear I didn't..."

"Don't talk tripe, Teddy," Brent interrupted gruffly. "If it comes to that, I was a medical student once myself."

They all turned their eyes on Brent as he spoke, and from him to Sir Anthony as he rose to his feet and confronted Teddy.

"Fraser," he boomed. "Where were you when Kay saw you, eh?"

Teddy thought for a moment before replying.

"Across the hall," he said, "near the surgery door."

"Which is next door to the study, eh?"

"Anthony...my dear...surely..."

Sir Anthony silenced his wife with a wave of his hand, and fixed his eye upon the wilting Teddy.

"And you'd been there half an hour, eh?" he continued.

"I dunno—I suppose so."

"Trying to pick the lock, eh?"

"Yes."

"With what?"

Teddy fumbled in one of his pockets and drew out a penknife.

"With this," he said. "I wasn't actually..."

"You're quite sure it was with that, eh?" Sir Anthony had put on his cross-examining voice and manner again.

"Why not?" Teddy looked puzzled.

"How many carving-knives are there in this damned house? Anybody know, eh?" Sir Anthony wheeled round on the others as he put his question.

"Are you suggesting, Father, that Teddy killed Manning?" Kay put the question with some of her special brand of sarcasm.

"Somebody killed him," boomed Sir Anthony, "and Fraser here says he was messing about right outside the study door for half an hour, and he was a medical student once." He turned again to Teddy with such suddenness that the latter jumped. "Would you know how to stick a knife in a man so that it killed him instantaneously, Fraser?"

"Look here, Sir Anthony," interrupted Brent. "This sort of thing can't do any good at all."

"Of course it can't," Kay supported him. "If Teddy had killed Manning—and believe me, he would go up in my estimation if he had..."

"Kay...my dear..."

"Do you think he would tell you?" finished Kay, "Father, as a Sherlock Holmes you're rotten."

Sir Anthony was about to frame an angry retort when the door opened and Tony entered the room. He was pale to the lips, and his young face was strangely drawn. He stood just inside the door which he closed quietly behind him, and faced them for a moment in silence.

"Tony!" Kay took a step towards him. "What on earth's the matter? Why are you looking like that? Has anything happened to Helen?"

Tony shook his head, and they saw that he was biting at his lower lip. He looked towards Brent, and it was to Brent that he spoke, raising his head as he did so.

"Bill," he said, "when can the police come?"

Lady Fane gave a little gasp.

"The police? Tony…my dear…"

Brent rose to his feet.

"Why, Tony?"

Tony looked down at his hand which he was clenching and unclenching nervously.

"The fact is," he began haltingly, and paused. Then he put his head up, and continued firmly: "I killed Manning."

Chapter Nine

Nine to Ten

LADY FANE WAS THE FIRST TO RECOVER FROM THE shock of Tony's sudden and dramatic announcement. With a whimpering little cry she jumped out of her chair, ran to him, and flung her arms about his neck.

"Tony…my dear…my dear… Say you didn't do it… Tell me I'm dreaming…"

Tony unwound his mother's arms and put his own around her. He bent his head over her, patted her on the back, and led her gently back to her chair into which she subsided weeping. Straightening himself, he faced Brent again, and waited for the latter to speak. But Brent could only stare in dismay.

"Well?" asked Tony presently, looking from one to another of the other three.

Sir Anthony let out a deep breath and stepped towards his son.

"Are you serious, eh?" he asked in a whisper.

Tony faced his father squarely.

"Perfectly," he answered shortly.

"Then I'll be damned!" Sir Anthony backed to the empty chair at his wife's side and dropped heavily into it.

"I'm—I'm sorry to—to shock you all like this," said Tony, one hand at his tie.

Kay came across from the windows to her brother's side and held out her case to him.

"Have a cigarette, old thing," she said, and when he accepted one from the open case, she struck a match and held it until the cigarette was alight. "Mother," she continued, turning to Lady Fane who was commencing to sob, "you'd better go and lie down. Take her upstairs, Father."

But Sir Anthony seemed past understanding, and then, surprisingly enough, Lady Fane rose to her feet and went herself to the door. Tony followed her with his eyes, and as she reached it, he ran after her, and, putting his arms about her, gave her a little hug before he opened the door for her to pass through. His face, as he turned back into the room, was more drawn than ever, and he blinked his eyes fiercely, as if to keep back tears.

"Hadn't somebody better go and look after Mother?" he said unsteadily. "Kay..."

But Kay took no notice of his hint. Instead, she went back to her position at the windows.

"Do you expect us to believe that?" she asked over her shoulder, and at her unexpected question, Sir Anthony raised his head from his hands and looked up.

"What d'you mean, eh?"

Kay turned round and looked at Tony.

"Only that I don't believe a word of it," she said. "I don't believe that Tony killed Manning. That's what I mean."

"But, dammit! He said he did." Sir Anthony's voice was recovering. "You heard him, didn't you, eh?"

"Father!" Kay almost laughed outright. "Tony!" She went again to her brother. "What's the big idea?"

"There isn't any big idea, Kay," he replied. "I oughtn't to have barged in here like that"—his hand was teasing his tie furiously—"I didn't think—I mean I didn't want to upset Mother like that. Hadn't you better go up to her, Kay?"

"Mother'll be all right for a few minutes. I'll go up presently and stay with her. Now then"—her voice became brisk—"why did you come in here and say such a ridiculous thing?"

"It isn't ridiculous. At least, I don't see anything ridiculous in it."

"So you killed Manning?"

Tony nodded. The others looked on, and when Sir Anthony would have interrupted, he laid a warning hand on his arm.

"I have just said I killed him," Tony replied.

"And now," continued Kay, "will you tell us why you should wait until now to say so?"

"Why not? I mean it's as good a time as any other." Tony glanced sideways at his sister. "What are you getting at, any-how?" he asked.

"You'll see in a minute. Just you answer my questions. When did you do it? I mean kill Manning?"

Tony shuffled his feet and thought before replying.

"I don't know the exact time," he replied, haltingly. "Some time between one and two, I suppose. Or it may have been just after two,"

"I see." Kay lit another cigarette before putting her next

question. "You came downstairs, I suppose," she continued when her cigarette was alight, "and went into the study?"

"Yes."

"Well, tell us what happened then. What was Manning doing at the time?"

"He was sitting at his table writing."

"Well?"

Tony shuffled his feet again, and Kay repeated her "Well?"

"Look here, Kay," said Tony, ceasing his shuffling and looking up at her, "what the devil's the good of going into all this? I told you I killed Manning; isn't that enough?"

"If you expect me to believe you, old thing, you'll have to do a bit more than that."

"Well, I don't care a damn whether you believe me or not."

"I see."

Kay smiled mysteriously and gazed at the tip of her cigarette as she flicked the ash off it.

"What d'you see?"

"Tell me"—Kay turned suddenly to him. "Where did you come from just now—when you came in here and made your announcement?"

"I'd been upstairs sitting by Helen's bed. Why?"

Tony stared with sudden understanding at his sister who was looking at him with a curious little light in her eyes.

"I understand," said Kay softly, and again she turned away and went to the windows.

"Then I'll be damned if I understand," declared Sir Anthony.

"There's nothing to understand," said Tony. "If Kay wants to know everything that happened, I'll tell you." His voice sounded almost eager, and all the hesitation had gone from his manner. "I found Manning sitting at his table writing. We had words…"

"Words? About what, eh?"

"Well, about the way he had been treating Helen."

"What d'you mean by that?"

"As a matter of fact, Helen had told me that she was afraid of him. She—she begged me to take her away from here, and—and—well, you all saw how he behaved last night at dinner. Helen was a nervous wreck, and has been for days." He paused before continuing. "Well, he told me then that he'd been leading us all up the garden about the engagement, and that he didn't mean to go through with it. So"—Tony shrugged his shoulders—"I killed him."

"Not a bad yarn, on the whole," said Kay mockingly, from the window. "You're a rotten liar, Tony."

"But I tell you it's the truth."

"Just a minute." Brent went to Tony's side and touched him on the shoulder. "You say you went down there to kill him?"

"Yes."

"Then you must have had the knife with you?"

Tony nodded quickly. "Yes, of course," he said.

"And where did you get it from?"

"Get it from?"

"Yes. Where did you get the knife from?"

"Well—I got it from the dining-room table where Kay said Mrs. Geraint had put it."

"You went in there, then, before you went to the study?"

"Yes. I went there to look for something to kill him with."

Kay snorted loudly, and Tony, now thoroughly roused, glared across at her.

"Look here, Kay..." he began, and into his face there came a terrible fear as he saw the understanding in her eyes. "You shut up, d'you hear? I swear, I'll..."

"What's all this, eh?" Sir Anthony glared from his son to his daughter. "What's all this about? What are you hinting at, Kay?"

"I was only wondering," began Kay quietly, and Tony ran across the room to her and would have put his hand over her mouth, but she stepped back.

"All right, old thing," she said. "I won't say anything."

She turned on her heel and went to the door.

"I'll run up and look after mother," she said as she went out.

"Now what does she mean by that, eh?" demanded Sir Anthony.

Brent, who had been following the exchange of words between Tony and his sister closely, supplied the answer.

"Kay was wondering what Helen had been saying up in her room when Tony was there. Wasn't she, Tony?"

Tony turned on him, white to the lips again, furious.

"Bill, if you dare suggest that what Helen said in her delirium..."

"I haven't suggested anything," said Brent quietly.

"You mean he's shielding Helen, eh?" It had dawned on Sir Anthony at last.

"It won't wash, old boy," said Brent kindly, laying a hand on Tony's shoulder. The latter sank into a chair and covered his face with his hands. "Nobody's going to take any notice of what Helen said," continued Brent.

Tony shook his hand off and jumped to his feet.

"I tell you all," he said loudly, "that I killed Manning. I had a sufficient motive for it, and I am prepared to give myself up to the police as soon as ever I can get out and do so. And that's that!"

The door opened quietly, and Henderson appeared around it.

"I've ordered some food for everybody," he said in his gentle voice, and then, noticing the strain on everybody's faces, "What's the matter here?"

"Tony here's been telling us he killed Manning," Sir Anthony replied for them all, "and we think he's shielding Helen."

The doctor stood stroking his chin with his hand as he absorbed this information. Presently, he took his hand away, and nodded his head, a smile playing about the corners of his mouth.

"Well, well!" he said. "There'll be plenty of time for us to go into that. Let's go and have some breakfast."

Chapter Ten

Nine to Ten (Continued)

"Food, eh? Breakfast?"

Henderson nodded.

"Bacon and eggs," he replied, "and coffee. I'm afraid there's no fresh milk, and only yesterday's bread; but it all smells very good. It's laid in the dining-room. Come along; it will do you good."

He held the door open for them, and with a grunted "Well, I suppose one may as well, eh?" Sir Anthony passed out into the hall, followed by Brent and Teddy Fraser.

The doctor looked at Tony who had remained staring moodily at the floor, his hands thrust into his pockets.

"What about you, Tony?" he said presently.

The boy looked up and shrugged his shoulders.

"Don't feel much like eating," he replied.

Henderson closed the door and sat down on the nearest chair.

"Just as you like, of course," he said, "but a meal at the right time never does any harm. Got a cigarette?"

Tony fumbled for his case and brought it over to the doctor

who selected a cigarette and lit it in silence. He puffed away at it with the awkwardness of the confirmed pipe-smoker, and watched the boy as he strolled slowly across to the windows.

"What exactly did Helen say, Tony?"

The other wheeled round quickly at the question, all moodiness gone from his face.

"What d'you mean?" he asked.

Henderson took the cigarette from his mouth and examined the burning end.

"When you were alone with her just now," he replied. "When I had to go and see to Mrs. Geraint. What did she say?"

For a moment Tony stared at his questioner, his face full of doubt and fear, then he came and stood over the doctor.

"What should she say?" he demanded. "What exactly are you getting at, Hendy?"

Henderson looked up at the excited face of the boy and smiled kindly.

"There's nothing to get worked up about, my boy," he said. "I'm only trying to help you, that's all. What was it that she said?"

But Tony had evidently made up his mind.

"She said nothing at all," he replied sullenly.

"She wasn't even a little delirious again? Just for five minutes?"

"No."

"She said nothing at all, for instance, that made you think she might have killed her father herself?"

"Look here, Hendy..."

But the other rose to his feet and patted him on the shoulder.

"Let me advise you, Tony," he said quietly. "Don't persist in that confession of yours. It won't do any good at all, and there's no need for it. It's about as effective as Mrs. Geraint's confession."

"Mrs. Geraint?" Tony's voice was full of surprise. "Mrs. Geraint confessed?"

Henderson nodded. "Yes," he said, "you're not the only one who has confessed. Mrs. Geraint thought she did it because she dreamed she had killed him. You are trying to shield Helen because she dreamed she did it."

"What d'you mean?"

"My dear boy, I've been sitting at Helen's bedside most of the morning, and I know the sort of thing she's been raving about. You heard some of it, too."

He paused in the hope that the boy would say something, but Tony maintained his sullen silence.

"Suppose you persist in your statement, Tony," the doctor went on. "D'you think the police are going to be content with just that? That they won't find out everything that there is to be found out?" Again he paused, but the boy said nothing. "I just wanted to know," he continued, "what it was Helen did say which upset you so much while I was in Mrs. Geraint's room."

"I haven't admitted she did say anything." Tony broke his silence at last.

"Just as you like." Henderson turned to the door. "I don't want to worry you, my boy, but—well, I was thinking of your mother and father. It seems rather a pity to add to their worries, doesn't it?"

The doctor had opened the door, and was about to pass through into the hall, when Tony, as if suddenly making up his mind, placed his hand upon the old man's arm and drew him back into the room. He closed the door before he spoke.

"Tell me one thing, Hendy," he said, his hand working nervously at his tie, his lips trembling.

"Suppose we sit down?" Henderson led the boy to a chair and pushed him gently down into it. He drew up another and sat down himself. "Now what is it, Tony?"

Tony fidgeted in his chair, clasping and unclasping his hands nervously. The old doctor, having had plenty of experience of other people's nervousness in his time, waited patiently.

"You remember what Helen said last night," Tony said presently; "after that business in the laboratory?"

The doctor thought back to the scene of the night before. "You mean…?"

"When we were all in here, and Helen said—said he was mad; that she had known it for a long time."

"Well?"

"Don't you remember"—the boy became more nervous as he spoke—"how she tried to release me from the engagement because of it?"

Again the doctor paused before making any reply. He was anxious to make quite sure of what was in the other's mind. Tony, seeing his hesitation, went on:

"Wasn't it because she was afraid that she had—well, inherited his insanity?"

"I see." Henderson got up from his chair and prowled about the room. Tony watched him anxiously.

"Of course it isn't true, is it?" the latter asked presently.

"Is what true?"

"About Manning's being mad?"

"What has this got to do with that confession of yours?" The doctor was hedging.

"Don't you see?"—Tony rose excitedly to his feet—"they would lock her up for the rest of her life in that place—what do they call it?—Broadmoor. Fancy Helen locked up in a place like that for the rest of her life! Could you imagine it?" He plucked nervously at his mouth. "Why! I should go mad myself thinking about her there all through the years. I couldn't go on living… I couldn't really…"

"And so you thought you'd get yourself hanged instead, was that the idea?"

Tony stared at the old man. "Look here…" he began, but Henderson came and thrust him back into the chair, and smiled down on him.

"If that is what you are afraid of, Tony," he said, "you can take it from me that Helen has not inherited any insanity from her father."

"You mean that? You're not just…"

"I'll give you my word of honour if you like."

"Then…"

"Then what?" prompted the doctor as the other paused. But Tony did not continue his question.

"Delirious babblings," Henderson continued, "should never be taken seriously. They are made up of fears, old dreams, and all the junk stored away in the subconscious mind, just as often as of things which actually have happened. Anything which passed through the mind once, anything read, or overheard, or imagined, or feared can suddenly come back in delirium."

"You're sure?"

"I'm a doctor, my dear boy. It's my job to know these things, and if you'd heard some of the delirious raving I've heard in my time…" The doctor ended with a shrug of his shoulders, and contemplated with his kindly smile the doubt still in the young face before him.

"But she said she killed him."

Henderson drew in his breath with a little hiss, and Tony suddenly realising what he had let slip, jumped to his feet, his face whiter than before.

"I didn't mean that," he said hoarsely. "I take that back. She said no such thing, she…" He clenched one fist and drove it distractedly into the open palm of his other hand. "I killed Manning," he almost shouted. "I tell you it's the truth. I killed him. Helen had nothing whatever to do with it. You must believe it. You've got to believe me, d'you hear? I tell you if you don't promise to believe me, I'll—I'll shoot myself before the police come. I'll—I'll—oh, my God!"

The boy collapsed into the chair behind him and covered his face with his hands.

Again the old doctor's experience came to his aid, and he allowed the boy's paroxysm of grief and fear to have its way before he spoke.

"Very well, Tony," he said presently, in his soothing voice, "if you want it that way, then have it so. I won't interfere, I promise you."

Tony raised his white face from his hands.

"You swear that?" he asked.

"What is it you want me to swear?"

"That—that you won't tell anybody what I've just told you."

"I'll swear that."

"Thank God for that!" Tony pulled his handkerchief out

of his pocket and wiped his forehead. "That will take a great load off my mind," he added. He started up as if some new idea was troubling him. "What about Helen?" he asked.

"What about her?"

"Have you left anybody with her?"

"Nobody."

"She may talk again—have delirium, don't you understand? And if somebody else heard…"

The doctor shook his head.

"Helen won't be delirious again," he said. "I gave her a sleeping draught, and when she wakes from that she'll be all right. Nothing to be afraid of there. You can go and sit by her if you like."

Tony hesitated for a moment, then walked slowly to the door. The doctor watched him go, and, just as he reached out his hand for the knob, he spoke again.

"I should think over that confession, Tony," he said. "Don't say anything more about it for the time being."

The boy nodded. "Very well," he said heavily, as he went out.

The old doctor, left alone, continued to stare at the closed door with eyes which did not see it. They saw, instead, the face of the girl who slept so heavily in the room upstairs; a face colourless and lined with sudden terror and suffering; and, as he stood there, the lines about the old man's mouth and eyes seemed to deepen.

A full minute must have passed thus before the silence of the room was broken by a heavy sigh, and the sounds of slow movement as old Henderson sat down wearily in the chair into which he had, so recently, pressed Tony, and, in his turn, covered his bowed face with his hands.

Chapter Eleven

Ten to Eleven

THE MEAL IN THE DINING-ROOM HAD BEEN A SILENT ONE.

At first it had threatened to be no meal at all, for none of the three men appeared anxious to eat. It was Brent who was the first to approach the sideboard and help himself to coffee, and it must have been the sight of him sipping his steaming and fragrant cup which prompted Sir Anthony, and then Teddy, to follow suit and help themselves.

They sipped their coffee in silence for some time. Sir Anthony, going to the sideboard for a second cup, raised the lid of the dish of bacon and eggs, contemplated its tempting contents for some moments, and then helped himself liberally.

"May as well eat," he grunted as he bore his plate to the table. "No sense in not eating, eh?"

Brent looked at the bacon and eggs on Sir Anthony's plate and agreed.

"Come on, Teddy," he said, rising. "Come and help yourself, and for goodness' sake, buck up and don't look so miserable."

Teddy smiled feebly and helped himself to food.

"Do us all good, a good meal," barked Sir Anthony. "Where's Tony got to?"

No answer was forthcoming to this question.

"Lot a damn nonsense that confession of Tony's, eh?" Sir Anthony looked up at Brent who nodded his head.

"Yes," he said slowly. "He seems to have got it into his head that Helen was the guilty party."

"Question is," continued Sir Anthony, taking no notice of Brent's observation, "what's to be done next, eh?" He speared another piece of bacon and waved it about on its way to his mouth. "Seems to me, Brent, we ought to be doing something about it, eh?"

"What can we do?"

"Only thought," Sir Anthony went on, "that I'm a J.P. Just occurred to me, in fact!"

Brent shook his head.

"I don't think that imposes any responsibility upon you, Sir Anthony. We'd best wait until the police come, and when that's going to happen"—Brent looked over his shoulder at the windows—"God knows. It looks as bad as ever."

"Nobody we could send, eh?"

Again Brent shook his head.

"Even if there were," he said, "I'm sure the police wouldn't come through this. I wouldn't like to be the one to send anybody out in this racket, would you?" He sipped his coffee. "It's nearly twelve miles to the village, and from there they'd have to send to Frenting to the county headquarters. The local constable couldn't do anything very much."

"And when they do come," growled Sir Anthony, "they'll take hours questioning us."

Brent nodded.

"I shouldn't be surprised if we don't all spend another night in this house," he replied gloomily. "We're all under suspicion."

Sir Anthony glared.

"Lot of damn nonsense," he boomed. "Plain as a pikestaff to my mind. Either that woman did it, or Strange."

Brent shrugged his shoulders.

"Maybe," he said wearily. "Well, Strange is dead, so they won't be able to…"

The remainder of his sentence was drowned in the crash of crockery, and all three men jumped to their feet. Standing in the doorway was the maid Alice, her eyes wide-open and staring, her face a picture of amazement and terror. At her feet reposed the cause of the crash, a tray-load of crockery, amongst the ruins of which lay a further supply of bacon and eggs.

"What the devil, eh?" Sir Anthony barked at her. "What are you standing there for looking as if you'd seen a ghost, eh? Come on, speak up, girl."

"Strange, sir…" the girl managed to whisper.

Sir Anthony was about to boom again, and Brent stopped him just in time with a warning gesture.

"What about him, Alice?" he asked kindly.

"You said he was—was dead, sir." She still spoke in a whisper.

"Dead as mutton, my girl," replied Sir Anthony before Brent could prevent him. "In the study with Mr. Manning. What d'you know about it, eh?"

The girl continued to stare at them for another moment and then collapsed, leaning against the open door.

"Oh, my God! My God!" she gasped. "Dead! Dead!"

Brent left his chair and went to her, and as he did so, the girl pulled herself together with an effort, and stooped down to the mess on the floor at her feet.

"Didn't you know Strange was dead, Alice?" he asked.

The girl did not look up, but continued to fumble with the pieces of broken crockery.

"I—I didn't know," she murmured so low that Brent had to repeat his question. "No, sir," she answered a little more audibly.

"But didn't you see him—his body, I mean, in the study when Mrs. Geraint—er—?" He let it go at that and bent over her to catch her answer. He could see that her fingers trembled violently as they groped on the floor.

"No, sir. I—I only saw the master."

Brent straightened himself and hesitated on the brink of another question. The girl's agitation, her momentary collapse and then her successful effort at self-control, had roused in him a strong desire for further questioning, and a number of ideas flashed through his mind as he stood there. Alice was an attractive specimen of her sex, and conceivably the dead Strange had found her so, too. In which case she might perhaps have been in his confidence, and could tell them a lot which it might be good for them to know. She might, for instance, know if it was the formula which Strange was trying to steal, and what he was going to do with it when he got it.

But the moment was not right for any such examination. He would wait until he could get her alone.

"It's been a night of shocks for all of us, Alice," he said kindly.

"Yes, sir," she replied in little above a whisper.

"I shouldn't bother about it any more, if I were you. Try to put it out of your mind."

The girl rose from her stooping position, and without a word, hurried away. Brent returned to his chair, and was about to speak, when Alice returned to the doorway, a floor-cloth in her hand. In silence the three men watched her collect the broken crockery and clean up the mess of food on the floor. She was almost composed as she told them that she would go and prepare some more bacon and eggs.

Brent lit his pipe, and for some five minutes or so, the three men continued to sit in silence after the maid had left them. Then Brent, with an affectation of casualness, rose from his seat, murmured something about going up to his room, and left them.

Once outside the door his casual air left him, and, darting a look around the deserted hall, he slipped quickly through the door which he knew led to the kitchen, and closed it quietly behind him.

He made his way down the passage which he found himself in to the door at the end which opened into the large kitchen itself.

But the kitchen was deserted. He looked into the scullery beyond, and found this empty too. The door which, he expected, gave on to the garden outside, was locked on the inside, so, obviously, nobody had gone through it. What, then, had become of the maid who had said she was about to prepare more food?

As he stood there turning this question over in his mind, a wild idea struck him, and he hurried back the way he had come, taking what care he could as he passed into the hall again, to see that it was empty before he re-entered it. Then, with hurried steps, he crossed it to the study.

The key of the study was still in the door—a fact which, for a moment, made him pause and wonder. Then he remembered that he, himself, had been the last to lock that door, and that he had no more right to take the key into his possession than had anybody else.

With one final look round, he tried to turn the key in the lock, and his heart beat a little faster as he discovered that it would not turn. The door was unlocked.

With a quick turn of the knob he pushed it open, stepped quietly inside, and pushed it to behind him. Somebody who had been bending over the body of Strange at the other end of the room, stood upright with a rustle of skirts, and gasped loudly. It was, as Brent had expected, Alice.

She stood watching him with wide-open eyes as he advanced slowly into the room, around the table and the dead body of Manning, until he stood facing her over the body of the dead butler.

"What are you doing here?" he asked at last.

Her answer made him start with astonishment.

"What has that got to do with you?" she asked, and now there was no nervousness in her manner. On the contrary, her mouth had set into a firm little line, and there was a hard light in her eyes. "I have as much right here as you have, Mr. Brent," she continued.

Brent's astonishment increased, and for a moment the two continued to stare at each other over the dead body at their feet.

"Look here, Alice…" he began, when she cut him short.

"You have no right that I know of to ask me questions," she said, and Brent noticed that this time there was a little upward trend in her voice. She was not, after all, quite so self-possessed as she had seemed.

"Listen to me," he said firmly. "I come in here and find you, one of the maids, bending over a dead body. What more natural than that I should ask you what you are doing here?"

"And what if I refuse to answer?" The question was accompanied by a toss of the head.

"You can if you like, of course." Brent watched the girl's face carefully as he made his next remark. "I shall have to tell the police that I found you here," he went on, "and that you refused to explain your presence here. You won't have much option about answering them."

With a certain amount of satisfaction he noticed that the girl started as he mentioned the word police, and that, for a brief moment, her eyes dropped before his steady stare.

"Come, Alice," he pressed her, "don't be a fool. Tell me what you are doing here."

For some moments the girl hesitated. Then, presently, she raised her eyes to his again, and this time the light in them was distinctly one of defiance.

"I was looking, if you want to know," she said, "for something which belongs to me."

"What was it?"

She did not answer this, and Brent tried again.

"Was it something which Strange had?"

Again the girl refused to answer.

"What was Strange to you?"

The girl brought one hand from behind her back and

plucked nervously at her dress. Brent noticed that the other hand was kept carefully behind her. He waited for her to answer his questions, waited while she transferred her hand to her mouth, and gnawed at the nail of her thumb.

"If I tell you, Mr. Brent," she said presently, "will you keep it to yourself?"

Brent considered the request.

"I don't know," he replied. "I may not be asked about it." He looked up at the maid again. "In any case," he continued, "you can do yourself no harm by telling me. It will come out some time, and I may be able to advise you."

The girl thought again for some moments, and then appeared to make up her mind.

"I've done nothing wrong," she began, and Brent encouraged her with a little nod. "Mr. Strange and I were—were keeping company. We had an understanding."

"I see. You were going to be married?"

She nodded.

"Nobody knew that but ourselves," she continued. "It had to be kept secret because of—of—" she hesitated, looking away from Brent.

"Because of what?"

"Because of what had to be done, sir."

"And what was that?"

Brent had to wait patiently for his answer. But, bit by bit, the girl's composure and self-control was breaking down, and he began to feel confident that, with a little more patience and kind treatment, he would get the whole of her story from her.

"Let's sit down," he suggested, and then he suddenly remembered the company they were in, and realised that to invite a girl to sit down in the presence of a couple of corpses was not an ideal method of promoting her composure.

"We'd better go to some other room and talk," he said gruffly, and for the first time the girl showed relief. She turned away from him to the door, and Brent noticed, as she did so, that something was clasped in her right hand. He arrived at the door first, and turned to her as he seized the knob.

"Show me what you've got in your hand, Alice, before we go," he said with something of a return to his former firmness.

After a moment's further hesitation, the girl brought her hand slowly from behind her back and, holding it out to him, opened it. A little roll of pound notes lay in the palm.

"There you are, sir," she said. "That's my money. Fifteen pounds. You can count it if you like."

Brent took the roll and opened it. He did not count the money. He merely wished to make certain that there was nothing else there, and, having done this, he handed the money back to her with a little smile.

"All that fuss over that!" he said lightly. "Well, let's go somewhere where we can talk. What about the kitchen?"

She nodded, and Brent opened the door sufficiently to allow him to peep through it. Having ascertained that the hall was still empty, he pulled the door open, and followed the girl through it, turning the key in the lock behind him.

Chapter Twelve

Ten to Eleven (Continued)

"Is that coffee I smell?"

Brent closed the door of the kitchen and prepared a careful smile for the girl as she turned towards him.

"Why, yes, sir. It'll be boiling over by now." She hurried towards the scullery, and Brent, finding his pipe and pouch, called out after her.

"What about a cup each? I could do with another cup of coffee."

Alice returned to the kitchen bearing a steaming coffee-pot which Brent relieved her of, telling her to find two cups and saucers, and holding it until she fetched these from the dresser, with sugar, and an opened tin of condensed milk. He, himself, poured the hot coffee into the two cups, and then, having handed over the pot to her, he sat himself down and prepared to be agreeable.

"Now then, Alice," he commenced, lighting his pipe. "You don't mind my calling you Alice, do you?"

She looked up at him over the brim of her upraised cup and shook her head.

"You're quite right, of course," he continued easily. "I've got no earthly right to question you, but you understand, Mr. Manning's been murdered, Strange has died, and—well, here we are. It's natural, isn't it, that some of us should want to find out what we can before the police arrive?"

She nodded again and set down her cup.

"What we've got to do," he went on, "is to help each other. Sooner or later the police will arrive and—well, we'll all have to go through it."

"You mean they'll have us all up…?"

"And question us." Brent nodded. "You bet your life they will." He puffed at his pipe and, crossing his legs, settled himself more comfortably in his chair. "On the other hand," he resumed, presently, "if we can find out one or two things, then perhaps we can avoid all sorts of trouble. You see what I mean?"

Brent managed another smile at the girl who sat staring at him as though fascinated, and noted with satisfaction that the defiance had left her eyes.

"What is it you want to know, sir?" she asked.

"Let me tell you first," Brent replied, cunningly, "what I know about it." He took his pipe from his mouth and studied the glowing bowl. "At about four this morning," he continued, and his attitude was that of a man taking an esteemed colleague into his confidence, "I heard noises coming from the study, and I came down to see what was causing them. I found the windows open, Mr. Manning lying dead over his table with a knife in his back, and the study in the devil's own mess. About half an hour later, or thereabouts, we found Strange lying outside beneath a big bit of tree which had fallen on him, and we carried him back into the study, where he died. Then I discovered Mrs. Geraint sleep-walking, and I followed her down to the study. You know the rest of that incident. Then I find you in the study with Strange and Mr. Manning, and you tell me that you went there to get some money which belonged to you." He paused again to allow all this to sink in. The girl had placed the roll of notes on the table before her, and her fingers were playing with them. "Of course," he continued, "I'm perfectly certain there was nothing wrong in your going there, but you must see that it needs explaining." Again he paused before saying, off-handedly: "It's really no concern of mine, but, at the same time, I don't want to see anybody—er—well, you know what I mean?"

"I don't mind telling you everything, sir," said the girl after a considerable pause, and Brent nodded approvingly and encouragingly.

"Mr. Strange has been making up to me for some time now…"

"I can quite understand that," interrupted Brent.

"And we had an understanding," continued the girl with a faint blush.

"You mean he had proposed to you?"

"Yes, sir. We were going to get married as soon as—as— the business about the formula was over and finished with."

Brent pricked up his ears at this, but managed to conceal the surprise with which her words had filled him. He waited in silence for her to continue, which she did.

"He told me, sir," she went on, "that Mr. Manning had made a big discovery which was so important that our Government had to get hold of it at all costs, and that the master was going to sell it to the Germans if we didn't prevent him. Mr. Strange was a Government Secret Service agent, you see, and he was only trying to get the secret for our country, and the only way he could do this was to steal it, and that was what he was trying to do last night, and he said he was going to run away and that I was to follow him this morning."

She paused for breath.

"Where to?" asked Brent.

"To London," she replied, "and we were going to be married there as soon as he had handed over the secret to the Government. I went down and bought a ticket to London yesterday after lunch, and I gave Strange all my money to keep for me."

Brent's eyebrows climbed up his forehead at this extraordinary tale. He began to see light as the girl went on with it.

"I had to meet a Mr. Jenkins there," she said, "and give him an envelope which Strange was going to give me last night, and this Mr. Jenkins was to take me to meet him. Then we were going to be married."

"And what, did you suppose, was to be in the envelope?"

"A letter," the girl replied readily. "Mr. Jenkins was a friend of Strange's, and he was just going to look after me till I found Strange."

"I see! And what was Strange going to do in the meantime?"

"Hand the secret over to the Government."

Brent pondered this last reply in silence. He thought he could understand Strange's plan from what he had heard. The simultaneous disappearance of the girl and himself would, in the first place, provide a crossed trail, and there could be no doubt upon which trail the hunt would be hottest for the stolen formula. A simple, and quite a clever plan on the whole. The subsequent disappearance of Mr. Jenkins, and the difficulty of proving that the letter the girl had handed him did really contain the missing formula, or a copy of it, would have been no small one.

"And you went into the study just to get that money back?" he asked presently.

"And the secret," the girl replied. "I was just as keen as Strange was to get it into the hands of our own government."

She looked so determined and patriotic as she said this, that Brent could only marvel at her simplicity and credulity. He asked her one more question.

"And what would you have done with it if you had found this secret?"

"Taken it to Mr. Jenkins," she replied promptly.

"Have you ever met him?"

"Oh, yes." Alice was evidently pleased at the impression she was sure she was making, for her replies became more assured. "I met him one afternoon in Frenting with Mr. Strange. He used to write letters to me for me to give to Mr. Strange, and that was how they communicated with each other without anybody being any the wiser."

Brent scratched his head as much in amazement as perplexity. He had often read of the credulity of women and girls in the hands of such scoundrels as Strange evidently had been, but this was the first instance of such cases he had personally come across. Alice really believed that she had been engaged in a bit of patriotic secret service work. He rose to his feet.

"Well," he said, "I'm glad you told me all this, Alice. It helps a great deal, and if you tell your story to the police as clearly and well as you have told me, then you'll have nothing to fear."

She rose, too, from her chair.

"I've got nothing to fear, sir," she said earnestly. "I don't know what happened, or why Strange was killed like that, or what's become of the secret…"

"I dare say we shall all know all about it in good time," he replied, cutting her short. "I'm just as much in the dark about it as you are," he added with a smile as he pulled open the kitchen door.

Chapter Thirteen

Eleven to Twelve

Brent went back to the dining-room which, thankfully, he found empty, and sat himself down in a deep chair.

The storm outside continued. The thunder had ceased over an hour since, but it had given way to a wind of gale speed and force, and the rain was coming down as heavily as ever.

But Brent's mind was not occupied by the weather. It was concerned exclusively with the extraordinary series of events which had occurred since four o'clock that morning, and in his methodical way, he now proceeded to sort them out in as orderly a manner as his memory would permit.

Once again he went over, first of all the evening before, commencing with the dinner party. What, he asked himself, had Helen meant by her defiant declaration to her father that she was going to be happy at all costs? Did that mean that she had some reason to suppose that he—her father—meant to see that she was not going to be so? And suppose Tony knew of such a circumstance? Would not that give some colour to his own story about his interview with Manning during the night? It certainly fitted in.

On the other hand if, as Kay had clearly hinted, Tony was shielding Helen, why should he have suddenly chosen that moment to make his declaration of guilt unless it was that he had heard something Helen had said while he was watching at her bedside? Tony or Helen, then? Or perhaps both; in which case the confession of Tony would still be an effort on his part to exculpate a guilty partner, or one who was accessory after the fact. Here was an idea. Suppose Tony really had killed Manning; that the killing had either been witnessed or discovered by Helen, and that the sight or discovery had proved too much for her and had broken her down to collapse and subsequent delirium? Would not Tony, seeing the danger of involving her, want to clear her completely by making his confession straight away? Quite possible.

But there was the definite assertion of Henderson's that the blow had been delivered either with trained skill and knowledge, or with extraordinary luck. Which meant that, had Helen or Tony been responsible for it, then the one of them had experienced the great luck.

There was, again, the case of Mrs. Geraint who had, in her sleep, almost reconstructed the crime. But, on consideration, Brent decided that it would have been impossible for the housekeeper to have achieved such a result without evoking a sound from the victim, and here again, it would have to have been a case of extraordinary luck. Had not Henderson said, too, that the shock of the impact of the knife with the body would have awakened her?

Alice's story seemed straightforward enough. It was too extraordinary in itself to have been made up. There was, of course, the possibility that Strange had killed Manning; but Brent was disinclined to this theory on the ground that it was unlikely that the man would have remained in the house for over two hours after doing so.

No; unless Manning had been asleep at the time of the killing, then whoever had done it must have been in a position to enter the study and remain there without causing any audible demonstrations from the victim. Further, the killer must have been able to go behind Manning without exciting comment from that gentleman.

Take the knife. If it was the same one as Kay and Fraser had seen in Mrs. Geraint's hand, then, for some time it had lain exposed to view upon the dining-room table. It might not, of course, have been the same knife, but Brent was inclined to believe that it was; for the knife from the table had disappeared after Kay and Fraser had seen it placed there. They were the only two, as far as was known, who knew that the knife had been placed there. Somebody had removed it subsequently, and, more than likely, that somebody had inserted that same knife into Manning's back.

Kay and Fraser? Brent shuddered as the first of these names entered his thoughts; but she had to be considered with the rest, and he resolutely set himself to do so.

Kay had, undoubtedly, been worked up the night before in the laboratory and, had she had a knife in her hand when she confronted the scientist after the death of the kitten, he—Brent—felt quite sure that something untoward might quite easily have happened. He knew Kay; knew how deep her sudden anger could be and how uncontrolled were her impulses at such moments.

Fraser, too, had been upset; must, in fact, have been exceedingly upset, for, had he not even found his way downstairs in the middle of the night and spent half an hour trying to pick the lock of the laboratory in the vague hope of releasing the cats? This adventure might, of course, have been undertaken with a view to impressing Kay.

Brent tried to imagine the two sitting in the drawing-room. Kay would, he felt sure, have wanted to know what Fraser was doing down in the hall at that time of night, and his explanation would, perhaps, turn the conversation on Manning and the kittens. Or, and perhaps this was more feasible, they might have decided to return to the attack on the laboratory door together, and have picked up the carving-knife from the dining-room table on their way as a better instrument with which to open the locked door. Then—Brent's imagination was running away with him, and he almost saw what he thought—suppose they were disturbed by Manning coming out of his study? What would happen? They would, quite likely, adjourn to the study, all three, where Manning would enjoy their discomfiture and gloat over their misery and unhappiness at the fate of the unfortunate cats. Would it not be quite possible for Kay to move behind his chair with the knife in her hand, and then, in a moment of ungovernable rage, to strike?

Brent shuddered again as the complete idea occurred to him. It all seemed so plausible. It was, in fact, not only plausible, but possible; for would they not quite naturally return to their seats in the drawing-room and talk it over until they both fell asleep?

Brent jumped to his feet, his mouth set in a grim line. The more he thought over this imaginary sequence of events, the uglier did they seem and the more easily did they fit in. Not being a trained detective, he did not realise that it is one of the elementary rules of detection that facts must come before reconstruction, and not vice versa; that to think of a theory first and then fit facts to it, is exactly how not to go about solving a crime problem.

But the facts themselves were disturbing enough. Tony had confessed to the murder; Helen had also confessed to it (or so Brent firmly, and rightly believed) in her delirium; Kay and Fraser were, by their own admission, downstairs at the time the crime must have been committed, and they both knew where the knife was to be found. All four were young, and the creatures of youthful impulse; all four hated and feared Manning in varying degrees. The motives applicable in the cases of Tony and Helen, were, perhaps, stronger than those to be attributed to the others, but this fact was counterbalanced by the knowledge connected with the knife, and the fact that these others were downstairs at the time.

The more Brent thought about it, the less able was he to eliminate the four young people as he had already eliminated Strange and Mrs. Geraint.

Then suddenly he had an idea. He would go to the study himself and make as thorough an investigation of the scene of the crime as he could. Some vague thought of clues flitted through his mind, and he reflected, as he made his way thither, that several people having already entered the room and moved about in it and touched things there, he would not, probably, do any very great harm.

Chapter Fourteen

Eleven to Twelve (Continued)

BECAUSE THE CURTAINS WERE DRAWN OVER THE WINdows the room was in semi-darkness, and Brent switched on the light after he had carefully closed the door behind him.

He stood for a while surveying the scene before him, allowing his eyes to pass slowly over each detail of the room which was visible to him.

The big writing-table was, nearly enough, in the centre of the room, and facing the end at which he stood; in other words, Manning's chair was so arranged that, when seated at his table, his back would be towards the windows—in which position his body now was. Beyond him, in the space between his chair and the windows, lay the half-stripped body of Strange with the handkerchief still over the face. The coat, waistcoat, shirt, collar, tie, and vest which they had taken off him, were arranged on the seat of a chair near the windows. Directly opposite these latter, and in the centre of the wall on his right as he stood, was the safe with its false door hanging open.

At his feet the floor between the wall on his right and the table was littered with papers and books. Most of these had fallen from the table: some of the books had been pulled out of a bookcase below the safe. Very likely, Brent thought, unless the murderer had worn gloves, his finger-prints would be plentifully strewn over the covers of these books—unless, of course, this chaos had been created entirely by Strange.

Brent tried to reconstruct the crime.

The murderer, according to his theory, had entered through the door as he had just done, and would have been seen immediately by Manning who sat facing it. That meant that, being in full view of his intended victim, he must have managed to conceal the big carving-knife about him. It meant, also, that he must have been well known to Manning who would, otherwise, have shouted, or made some noise with a view to attracting assistance. The knife, Brent decided after a moment's consideration, might have been quite easily slipped inside the waistcoat, and held in position by the pressure of a buttoned coat—still more easily so if that coat had been a dinner jacket, which is usually fairly tight-fitting about the waist. The concealment of the knife presented no obstacle to the success of his reconstruction.

Having made his entry, the murderer, in the course of conversation, might have walked about the room, eventually working himself into a position directly behind the man at the table, and once there, it was simply a matter of choosing his moment to strike.

Brent tried to picture in his mind the actual striking. Obviously, at the moment of the blow, Manning must have had his face to the door, for he had fallen squarely on to the table with both his legs straight before him and beneath the table, and here was another, if unnecessary proof that the killer was somebody well known to the dead man. The blow was then delivered, and here Brent encountered his first difficulty. How would Manning be seated as the blow actually fell? Would he be sitting well back in his chair conversing? No, because—and to verify this, Brent had to take up a position at the side of the chair—the back of the chair would have prevented the knife from entering the body. Perhaps slightly forward then, and away from the back of the chair? Very likely. But no, that position, too, was impossible, as an examination of the angle at which the knife had entered the body proved. The handle of the knife stood at a wide angle to the line of the back, an angle of probably some eighty degrees, and in order to permit of this, Manning must have been sitting with his trunk bent well forward over the table, and the striker must have been standing quite near him, if not over him. Suppose they were both looking at something before them on the table. That was it!

Brent felt a little thrill of excitement run through him as this conclusion forced itself suddenly and almost unexpectedly upon him. He felt that he was making real progress.

Another little quiver of excitement made itself felt as he realised immediately that the striker must have been standing on the left side of the body. The back of the chair was too high to permit of the possibility of his striking effectively from directly behind; the right side of the body was ruled out unless the murderer was left-handed.

Left-handed? Brent pulled himself up with a shock. There was only one left-handed member of their company, and that was Kay. What about the knife, though, in her case? Where would she have concealed it? He recalled the dress she had been wearing, and realised with another shock that such a knife might easily have been concealed in its breast—more easily there, in fact, than in a man's waistcoat.

He paused, lost in thought, as these disconcerting ideas occurred to him; then, presently, he took up a position at the right side of the chair, bent over the body, and went through the actions of withdrawing a knife from the centre of his waistcoat. Yes, it could have been done quite easily. His arm stretched out over the body above the spot where, he estimated, the point of entry would have been in the live body, and brought it down with a short thrust. Yes, it could have been so done by somebody who was left-handed.

Standing at the same side, he went through the motions again, using his right hand this time, and found that, to make an effective stroke, he had to turn his own body towards the left to allow his right arm to stretch over far enough. This, too, would mean that the blade of the knife would enter with its edge pointing towards the neck, or the seat, whereas it had done no such thing. The broad side of the blade had entered in a line parallel to the shoulders.

He went to the other side of the body and, assuming that the knife was concealed in the left side of his waistcoat, he went through the same motions again. This time it worked fairly easily—as easily as the left hand had worked on the other side with this little difference, that the victim must have been bending very low over whatever was on the table.

Slightly relieved in his mind, Brent next turned his attention to the table itself.

The head of the dead man was lying on what appeared to be an open album. Brent cleared away the loose papers which almost covered that part of it not occupied by the head, and examined with interest the portraits which he could see. They were of a woman, startlingly like Helen; so like her, in fact, that they might have been pictures of her. But the prints were faded, and must have been taken some time ago. Helen, furthermore, did not wear her hair quite like that of the woman in the photographs.

As he stared down at the portions of the prints he could see, Brent noticed another curious thing. A bottle of red ink had been upset on the desk, and although the edges of the pages had been stained, no stain appeared on the top page. Which meant, he concluded with another little thrill of excitement, that this top page must have been turned over after the killing.

A moment's hesitation, and he decided that, at all costs, he must see the page underneath, if only to confirm his theory, and with this decision came the uncomfortable realisation that, in order to achieve this, he must raise the dead head sufficiently to allow him to turn the page.

With a slightly paler face, and his breath held, Brent bent over the body and, slipping his right hand beneath the cold forehead, he lifted it sufficiently to allow his left hand to turn back the page.

He had been right. The red ink had spilled over this page; but there was another, and still more exciting discovery to be made. From the centre of the page a portrait had obviously been torn, and torn after the ink had spilled; for the portion of the page where the portrait had been was innocent of ink.

This, then, was the page they had been looking at when Manning had been killed. Probably, the missing portrait had been absorbing their attention and absorbing Manning's to such an extent that he had bent low over it—low enough to enable his slayer to drive the knife at almost right angles into his body. If that portrait could be found...

Brent drew back from the table, wondering whether or not to lift the head again, and turn back the page he had disturbed. He decided eventually against this, and contented himself with restoring the pieces of paper to their position on the open page.

He then went to the other side of the chair where he dropped to his knees to examine the floor directly beneath the body. There was nothing of apparent importance there. The blood had dried upon the carpet, most of it covered by the contents of the drawers of the table which Strange had pulled out and dropped there. Brent stared at these intently with the vague hope of receiving some sort of impression from them, but he got nothing at all, and he placed one hand on the paper-strewn floor near his knees preparatory to rising to his feet again. As he did so, his hand moved one of the sheets of paper and touched something soft. Brent looked down. It was a tiny piece of material, and he picked it up, rising to his feet as he did so.

It was a woman's handkerchief, one which, had he not already recognised it, bore an embroidered initial in one corner which would have left him in no doubt as to its ownership.

It was Kay's. It was, furthermore, on the right side of the chair, just where she would have stood had she...

Brent stared at it with dismay and fear at his heart. Then the door opened, and he looked up to find Teddy staring at him.

Chapter Fifteen

Eleven to Twelve (Continued)

BRENT'S HAND CLOSED OVER THE SCRAP OF LACE, AND as he turned to face the boy at the door, he thrust it casually into his trouser pocket. It flashed through his mind that he would have given all he possessed to know if the other had seen exactly what it was he had held in his hand.

Fraser hesitated for a moment at the door which he still held open, then he stepped into the room and closed it behind him.

Each waited for the other to speak. It was Fraser who, at last, broke the silence.

"I didn't know," he said unsteadily, "there was anybody here."

Brent considered him before he answered this remark, and as he did so, there entered his mind a thought which drove the colour from his cheeks. It was a momentary mental picture of Fraser seated on one side of the table by which he stood, facing Manning who sat opposite, while Kay stood at the side—just where he, himself, stood now. The picture came and went in a flash.

"What did you come here for?" he asked, and he found it necessary to clear his throat which felt suddenly full.

"If it comes to that," returned Fraser, "how about you? I mean to say—well!"

"I came here to have a look around," said Brent.

"Just what I came for," said Fraser, and as he spoke Brent noticed that his eyes searched the floor near where he stood.

"What were you going to look for?" persisted Brent.

"Oh, I dunno." Fraser shuffled his feet and looked more uncomfortable than ever. "Curiosity," he finished, lamely enough. "No objection, I suppose?"

Brent thought for a moment. He had to confess that Fraser, or, for that matter, anybody else, had as much right in the study as he had.

"No, I've no objection," he replied. "Nothing to do with me, really, except that I suppose the room ought to be left empty for the police when they come."

Fraser's face turned a shade paler.

"The police, eh? Oh, of course, I forgot the police."

There fell a silence between them until Brent moved towards the door. Fraser stood on one side to allow him to pass.

"Aren't you coming?" Brent asked, turning to the other.

"Well, you know,"—Fraser shuffled his feet again—"thought I'd just have a look round. Clues, you know, what? I mean to say, jolly interesting all this, don't you think so?"

Brent hesitated, his hand upon the knob of the door; then suddenly he made up his mind.

"Nothing to do with me, of course," he said, with a shrug

of his shoulders. "I suppose I oughtn't to have been in here myself. See you later."

And with that he passed through the door, closing it behind him and made his way thoughtfully to the drawing-room. This was empty, and he stretched himself out on the settee, suddenly realising that he was tired.

His tiredness was, however, more mental than physical, and it being the kind of tiredness which would not allow him to rest, he was soon on his feet again, pacing up and down the room, turning over in his mind the discovery he had just made. His pacing became more and more rapid as he tried to puzzle things out. But he tried in vain, and he was no more successful when his thoughts turned to the future and what it might hold. The picture of Fraser, Manning, and Kay in that room persisted in his mind, and he began to curse aloud. Why had he gone there at all? Why not leave well alone?

A sound at the door made him pause and look up. It was Kay, and as he looked at her a sudden rush of tenderness almost overwhelmed him. He could have cried out with gratitude at the thought that that handkerchief lay safely in his pocket and not where he had found it on the floor beside the dead man.

Kay would have turned to go immediately, on seeing who the only occupant of the room was, but Brent strode towards her, a light in his eyes she had never seen there before, and she stood her ground and waited until he had come right up to her.

"Kay," he said, and there was no gruffness in his voice as he spoke her name. "Don't go yet. I must speak to you. Won't you stay for a moment?"

Kay stared at him in amazement, and then, pushing the

door to, she sauntered past him into the room and sat herself down on an easy chair.

"Well?" she said, not without a trace of hardness in her voice, "what can I do for you?"

"Look here, Kay, I'm most infernally sorry about that business this morning, and I've been waiting for an opportunity to say so."

Kay's plucked eyebrows climbed up her forehead.

"Dear me! And what business are you referring to?"

Brent came a step nearer.

"Don't play the fool, Kay darling…" He paused and flushed hotly as the word escaped him. Kay raised startled eyes to his.

"I'm terribly sorry," he stammered, his eyes now turned away from her, his face pale again. "I had no right to—to—I mean I forgot about Teddy for the moment."

Had he dared to look her in the face again, he would have seen a certain light in Kay's eyes which would have tumbled him down to his knees before her, but he did not do so, and the light, being wasted on the desert air, the moment was postponed. She said nothing, and he blundered on.

"Just consider it unsaid," he continued, and then, suddenly, he turned on his heel and marched up to the windows.

Kay stared after him, and this time the light was wasted on his broad shoulders as he stood with his back to her.

"The fact is," he resumed, presently, and speaking without turning about, "I want you to know that there's nothing in the world you can't ask me, no sacrifice you can't demand and—and receive."

He paused again, his back still towards her, waiting, perhaps for her to say something. But no sound came from her, and at last he turned about and faced her. What he saw brought him to his knees at her feet, for her head was bowed in her hands and she was crying quietly, stifling the sobs with her hands.

"Kay, my dear! Oh, my darling, don't cry like that. There's nothing to cry about. Leave it all to me. I won't let you down. I love you, don't you see, and you've got nothing to worry about—nothing at all. Just leave it all to me and forget it. I won't let the police come near you. There! Stop crying, stop…"

She raised a tear-stained face and stared at him with wet, bewildered eyes.

"G-g-got a handkerchief?" she asked, and Brent, before he knew what he was doing, had thrust his hand into his pocket and was dabbing at her face with her own handkerchief. He leaned back on his knees and stared with horror at what he had done. What a fool he was! Why couldn't he have remembered and given her his own handkerchief?

The horror deepened on his face as she held the handkerchief before her, straightening it in her two hands. Suddenly she looked more closely at it and raised her eyes to his.

"Where did you get this from?" she asked, and Brent mistook the astonishment in her voice for terror.

"Kay, my dear," he said earnestly, "I—I gave it to you by mistake. I—I didn't mean you to see it, but remember you've got nothing to fear—nothing at all. Just leave it all to me."

"But I don't understand you. What must I leave to you? And what's it got to do with this handkerchief? Where did you get it from?"

The perplexity in her voice and eyes was so genuine and unmistakable that he was taken aback.

"Why, I—I—" he stammered, and could get no further.

She studied his face through her tears, her perplexity growing with every moment.

"What's the matter with you, Bill?" she asked presently. "I don't understand a word of what you're saying. What is it I'm not to be afraid of, and what was that you said about the police?"

His amazement equalled hers.

"Don't you know what I mean?" he asked, and he rose to his feet as she shook her head.

"How should I know?"

He thought for a moment before replying to her last question. It was the continued amazement and perplexity in her face that decided him, at last, to tell her the truth.

"I found that handkerchief," he said, "just a few minutes ago."

"Where? I must have dropped it somewhere, I suppose."

"In the study," he continued.

"What? In the study? You mean in there—with—with—?"

Brent nodded.

"Near Manning's table. And, of course, I thought—well—what with one thing and another..." He did not finish the sentence because of the sudden embarrassment which surged up within him.

Kay finished it for him.

"You came to the conclusion that I had done the murder?"

Brent breathed hard through his nose.

"Well, I don't know about all that," he stammered. "I thought perhaps you and Teddy..."

He turned away from her again, unable to face her any longer. Somehow or other, he had managed to make a complete fool of himself. He, the clever detective who had found out so much from a few minutes' examination of the room! He almost laughed aloud. Fancy his dreaming for a moment that such a girl as Kay had committed such a murder!

He heard a sound behind him, and turned. Kay had risen from her chair and was waiting for him as he turned about. The lipstick had overflowed her lips, and there were dark streaks where the black colouring on her eyelashes had got mixed up with her tears. The hair, usually brushed so severely back from her forehead, had also rebelled and was hanging in curls over her temples. A tousled, tear-stained, discoloured but suddenly very feminine and soft Kay looked up at him.

Brent tried hard to return her gaze, but he felt suddenly weak and afraid in her presence, and once again his eyes dropped to the floor between them. He felt small and very foolish.

"So you thought I had killed Manning?" she asked in a curiously level voice.

Brent nodded.

"I suppose so," he said. "I'm sorry about it. I wouldn't have blamed you if you had, incidentally, but still…"

"Did you mean what you told me just now, or was it just that you thought I had done this thing and needed help?"

"Both."

"And I suppose you were going to do what that glorious fool Tony tried to do? Give yourself up and rush about confessing to everybody? Were you?"

"Well, I—er—I don't know about that, I—I hadn't thought very clearly about it, to tell you the truth, but as it's turned out, of course, there's no need for any—er—heroics on my part. I simply seem to have made a bigger fool than usual of myself."

"I see." Something of the old Kay was creeping back into her voice. "And I suppose now, that you'll go away somewhere and hide your secret sorrow beneath a stern-lipped smile for ever more, eh?"

Brent looked up and caught her old mocking gaze upon him.

"I don't see that there's all that to laugh at," he said stiffly.

"Don't you? But then, you can't see yourself, can you? And I can. But go on, do tell me what the programme's going to be? You'll commence, of course, by chucking up your job with Father, and then what? What's the modern equivalent to shooting lions? Or will it just be a case of drinking yourself to death in village pubs?"

Brent glared at her.

"Look here, Kay," he began, but she waved an imperious hand at him, and he dried up once more.

"Of course," she went on, thoroughly enjoying herself, "the confession idea was quite a good one, only you're a bit late. This house is crawling with confessions. It will have to be a triple hanging. You, and Mrs. Geraint and Tony. They'll probably put Mrs. Geraint between you two men. It will be sweet, won't it?"

Brent looked towards the door and would have stepped in that direction, but she side-stepped first, and he found his way blocked.

"Look here, Bill Brent," she said, folding her arms before her, and planting her feet astride. "I'm going to marry you. Oh, wait a minute," she continued, as he gasped, "you haven't heard the worst yet. I made up my mind to marry you about the second day you came to Fane Court, and let me tell you, you've never stood an earthly chance ever since. Get that?"

"Kay...you can't be serious?"

"Serious? Just you wait, my lad. You'll soon see if I'm serious or not."

"Kay, my darling…"

He stretched out his arms to her, and she went into them with a whispered: "Bill! Oh, my darling," and, a moment later: "Go easy, old thing, I've bust one of the bones in my belt, and if you're not careful, there'll be another death in the house. Phoo! Can the boy kiss?"

Neither of them heard the door open, and it was not until Brent released Kay from his embrace that they became aware that Teddy was standing in the open doorway, his face a mixture of amazement and misery.

"I'm sorry," he said, and was about to withdraw, when Kay ran to him and pulled him into the room, shutting the door as she did so.

"I'm sorry, too, Teddy dear," she said.

For a moment all three stood, at a loss for words, then Teddy pulled himself together and spoke to Brent.

"I—er—came to find you, Bill," he said.

Brent went to him, and laid a kindly hand on his shoulder.

"What is it, Teddy old man?" he said gruffly.

For a moment the other did not reply; then he raised his white face to Brent's, and cleared a full throat.

"It was about—er—I saw you pick up something in the study just now," he said.

"Was it this?" Kay interrupted him, holding out the handkerchief she held in her hand. Teddy took it from her and played with it in his fingers.

"Yes," he replied. "I must have dropped it there—in the study."

The others stared at him in amazement.

"You dropped it there?" It was Kay who put the question.

"Yes. I've been worried stiff. I've—I've been hunting all over the place for it, and—and the only place I hadn't been to was the study. I saw Bill pick up something there just now."

"But where did you get it from, Teddy dear?"

Teddy's face grew, if possible, whiter and more miserable than ever.

"The fact is I—er—pinched it from you last night," he said in a low voice, his eyes on the floor between them.

"But—but—" Kay's voice was still full of astonishment.

"The fact is," continued Teddy, "er—keepsake—I thought I'd like to—to—well…" His voice trailed off into silence.

"And you dropped it in the study?"

"Yes, I must have done so, I suppose. I—I couldn't find it anywhere else, and I was in there with the others when… when Strange was brought in."

Again there fell a silence between the three, then Kay took a step towards Teddy, saying as she did so:

"Look the other way, a moment, Bill."

Bill did not do so, and he saw Kay take Teddy's white face between her two hands, pull it down to hers until the two met in a kiss.

She released Teddy at last, and looked straight at Bill.

Her eyes were filled with tears. "One of the new detachable eyelashes," she explained, blinking hard.

Chapter Sixteen

Twelve to One

Sir Anthony was spending a miserable day. As the clock struck twelve he was engaged in stamping up and down the room which had been allotted to his wife and himself. Time and again he would stamp his way to the door, open it, and look out. Having satisfied himself that apparently nothing was happening in the house, he would stamp in again, slam the door and stamp over to the window through which he would look for a moment, before announcing in his loudest boom that the damned storm was still as bad as ever.

The unfortunate Lady Fane lay stretched upon the bed, where she had been ever since the scene in the drawing-room from which she had retired, and at which she had listened to her son's confession. Kay had come up to her, and sat by her side, holding her hand, until she had dozed off to sleep, in which happier state she had remained until her husband's arrival, after which all sleep became immediately impossible.

For the worthy and well-meaning baronet had made his arrival known to her by waking her up for the purpose of asking her if she felt better, and in response to her enfeebled moan of protest, he had sat down at her bedside, and assured her in his loudest voice that there was nothing the matter with her; that Tony was no more guilty of the murder than was he, Sir Anthony, and various other tit-bits of news, all of which he intended as information calculated to uplift and cheer his stricken spouse.

Having thus done his husbandly duty for some half-hour, he patted the prostrate lady firmly on her aching head, barked at her a gruff order to go to sleep immediately, and lighted a formidable cigar with which, the windows being shut on account of the storm, he proceeded to smoke her out. To all her feebly uttered protests, he boomed assurances that everything was, under his personal supervision, shortly to turn out perfectly all right and that all she had now to do was to go back to sleep and not to worry.

And presently Lady Fane sank into a sort of coma which was neither sleep not yet anything akin to it, but which had as one of its most prominent symptoms a distinct sensation of helpless nausea, and seeing her thus apparently composed if a trifle green about the face, Sir Anthony silently congratulated himself on his sick room methods, and proceeded to the further enjoyment of the remainder of his weed while he stamped up and down the space between window and door.

He heard the clock in the room strike the half and the three-quarters before anything occurred to disturb the monotony of his occupation and the enjoyment of a second—smaller—cigar, and the event took the form of an urgent knocking on the door.

In response to his bellowed invitation, Alice the maid

entered in a condition indicative of considerable agitation and breathlessness, and Sir Anthony, having favoured her with one of his celebrated stares, took his cigar from his mouth and let her have the full benefit of his lungs.

"Well?" he bawled. "What's the matter, eh? Come on now, speak up, don't stand there looking like that. Why, damn the girl, what's the matter with her, eh?"

He would probably have gone on like this indefinitely had not the maid whom he was addressing, suddenly put her finger to her mouth and a mysterious expression upon her comely countenance.

"If you please, sir," she whispered. "It's most urgent. The doctor's compliments, Sir Anthony, and will you please step down to the kitchen immediately. I was to say it is most urgent, and will you please to keep very quiet on the way down?"

This message was received with another glare, and an opening of the mouth which might have resulted in anything from a roar upwards, but it was checked again in time by the maid's agitated application of her finger to her mouth, and, without a word, the baronet followed her to the door through which she peeped still more mysteriously before she beckoned him to follow her through it.

Together they tip-toed down the stairs and across the hall, the maid ever and anon casting warning glances behind her at the mystified baronet whose effort to maintain silence was manifested by the swelling of various veins in his neck.

Without meeting anybody on the way, they reached the door which led out of the hall to the kitchen, and when this was closed, Alice stepped on one side, and remarked in a voice curiously loud, having regard to her previous insistence upon silence, that it would be as well if Sir Anthony led the rest of the way.

Sir Anthony stepped briskly into the lead, pushed the door at the end of the short passage open, and passed through it.

He had hardly done so when he became aware of a wet and slimy arm being placed about his neck from behind. At the same moment a large quantity of material was thrust into his mouth and kept there by another strip of material which was bound over it and tied with surprising tightness at the back of his neck.

Being unable to look down, he did not see the efficiency with which his legs were bound with still more material, and it may have been his overwhelming surprise at this reception which deprived him of the power to struggle even while his wrists were tied behind him.

He became aware, presently, of being lifted and dumped into a chair, to which he was firmly tied with still more material, and then of three figures clad in wet, green oilskins and wearing what looked like scarves over their faces up to the eyes, who stood in a row before him and surveyed him in silence.

Moving his head as far as he could to the left, he swelled visibly with astonishment as he caught sight of somebody else tied to another chair, and almost covered with the white bandages which were his bonds. With an effort, and by dint of concentrated study, he recognised the uncovered parts of the bound figure as belonging to Mr. Edward Fraser in whose eyes was reflected the amazement and furious anger which filled the baronet himself.

The sound of a very low-pitched voice speaking in some

language which he did not understand brought Sir Anthony's attention back to the three masked figures whose oilskins, he noticed, dripped water on to the kitchen floor.

Alice, who had stood in a corner of the kitchen, came forward at the sound of the voice, nodded, and said something in what sounded to Sir Anthony like the same language, and departed through the door to the hall.

And presently, when the three masked figures had taken up their positions each side of the door, all of them plentifully equipped with strips of white material which Sir Anthony now perceived to be sheets torn up for the occasion, there entered Tony who was promptly seized and trussed up with the same efficiency and speed as that which had characterised the binding of Sir Anthony.

Once more the same voice, the departure of Alice and the subsequent arrival of Doctor Henderson who, being an old and not very big man, was trussed up and bound to a chair in half the time; and his appearance was followed by that of Bill Brent who put up a magnificent fight and who was subdued only after some fifteen minutes' furious struggling.

But subdued he was, and once more Alice started off on her errand.

This time, however, the plan did not appear to be working quite to rule, for presently Kay appeared walking backwards through the door, her hands held above her head, and followed by the good-looking Alice who pointed a wicked-looking automatic at the girl's chest.

But once inside the room, Kay was soon reduced to impotence, and duly deposited on her chair from which she surveyed the remainder of the room with eyes wide with amazement.

There followed a whispered conference between Alice and the three masked figures, following upon which the maid once more disappeared, to reappear presently carrying Helen in her arms.

Helen's appearance was greeted with convulsive heavings on the part of Tony, seeing which, one of the three men approached him and examined his bandages, tightening them here and there with swift, silent efficiency.

The others watched anxiously while Helen was being dealt with, and Sir Anthony's amazement at these goings-on increased considerably as Alice, in obedience to a gruff order, disappeared again through the door to reappear presently with an armful of cushions which they proceeded to pack into the rocking-chair which was the exclusive domain of Mrs. Geraint.

The next to appear in the same way was Lady Fane, whom Alice appeared to be able to carry without any difficulty whatever, and who, on seeing the three masked figures, passed immediately into a convenient swoon, thus greatly facilitating the trussing-up performance. This, again, in her case, was achieved without roughness, but with none the less efficiency, a treatment in marked contrast to that received by Mary, the other maid, who was bundled into the kitchen, and strapped up in no time to a high-backed chair.

Finally, in response to a mouthful of unintelligible sounds, two of the three men accompanied Alice from the room, and all three returned presently, bearing the gagged figure of Mrs. Geraint, who was awake, and the flapping of whose arms was rightly interpreted by the others as protests of violent indignation.

The circle at last completed, the three men made a round of the bound figures and gave one final look to the bandages of each while Alice enveloped herself in green oilskins like the others.

The final scene of this little drama took the form of a short speech by one of the three men who spoke with a pleasant drawl, and without the slightest trace of accent of any description.

His words were short and to the point.

"I regret, ladies and gentlemen," he said, "this treatment, and believe me sincere when I assure you that we most earnestly hope that no harm will result to any of you from it. In very little time now, the storm will lift, and no doubt help will come, and you will be set free, little the worse for your experience."

He gave a little bow which comprehended the entire circle of bound figures, and in which his colleagues, Alice included, joined him, and then, without a word all four left the room through the door which led to the hall.

In the kitchen, silence reigned supreme.

Chapter Seventeen

One to Two

SILENCE DID NOT REIGN SUPREME IN THE KITCHEN FOR very long for the excellent reason that Sir Anthony, deprived temporarily of the use of his mouth, fell back upon his nose and developed through that organ a most impressive snort. With this he punctuated the silence at more or less regular intervals until he was compelled to take a rest, and to content himself with some very audible breathing.

Tony kept anxious eyes on Helen who slept on, propped with comparative comfort against the ample cushions which had been so thoughtfully provided for her. Mary and Lady Fane, both of whom dripped tears of fright and helplessness from their eyes, soon commenced a duet of sniffs, while Mrs. Geraint appeared to have passed into a condition of waking coma, for she sat, seeming hardly to breathe, and with unseeing but open eyes fixed steadily on the air immediately in front of her.

Mr. Fraser seemed to be more interested in his companions than in himself, for his eyes darted from one to another of them. Kay, alone of all of them, seemed to find the situation amusing. She sat next to her father, and at his every snort, she would wriggle her head sideways and survey him with dancing eyes. Brent, who sat opposite her was, presently bombarded with an astonishing series of expressions from his future wife's eyes; a series which developed into something as intelligible as a conversation. As he, himself, was to say subsequently, although he had frequently been assured by novelists of the existence of a language of the eyes, he had never believed in it until this day upon which he was compelled to sit opposite the bound and gagged Kay, and to be teased, flirted with, ragged, and made love to by a pair of eyes with which he had fallen in love, and yet, which he had never really understood and, therefore, never thoroughly appreciated before. Kay's demonstration of the language of the eyes was, unquestionably, an expert one, and no finer tribute could be paid to it than another remark of her husband's at a not very much later date, to the effect that, as long as his wife's eyes remained to her, it would hardly prove to be an affliction in her case if she did go dumb.

Old Doctor Henderson came out strong as a philosopher. But for an occasional glance around the circle of his companions, with perhaps a hint of anxiety in his eyes as they rested upon Helen, he sat in his bonds, a model of patient meditation. Now and again his eyes would wander to one of the others, dwell upon him or her for a few moments, and light up with encouragement, sympathy, or affection. Indeed, the character of the man whom everybody loved could have been read in those glances.

The angriest of them was, Sir Anthony not excepted, Brent. In the intervals of receiving, and endeavouring to return the stream of unspoken messages from Kay, he spent the time reproaching himself for the ease with which the plausible Alice had deceived him. He kicked himself mentally and blushed beneath his bandages as his mind went back to their conversation in the kitchen when he had adopted the kindly, paternal attitude, thinking himself so very shrewd in his treatment of her, and congratulating himself upon his success in getting her story from her. Alice, the unsophisticated country maid, apparently so easily deceived by the scoundrelly Strange, so very simple, so femininely inclined to hysterics; and this new Alice with the determined and cultured voice, with another language of her own, with complete mastery of herself, and so amazingly familiar with a pistol! Who was she? And where had her three companions sprung from?

He went over in his mind the conversation in the kitchen, and the story she had told him so artlessly, and with such an air of truth. Had he been present at another conversation, the one which had transpired between Strange and Manning on the afternoon of the day before, he would probably have come to the conclusion that her story was, actually, a very artful mixture of truth and fiction, and one which could, should subsequent circumstances demand it, be very thoroughly tested and not found wanting. The name of "Von Jenn," for instance, which Manning had mentioned, would have fitted in with her "Mr. Jenkins"; and, in all probability, this mysterious gentleman really had his headquarters under the name of Jenkins in Frenting. Brent would probably have concluded, also, that Strange—or, as Manning had called him,

Gibbons—was nothing more than a tool working under the expert and unsuspected supervision of the fair Alice.

And, as a final conclusion, Brent would certainly have decided that here, being enacted before his eyes, and in which he, himself, was taking a prominent part, was a bit of fact as strange as any fiction he had ever heard of; here was the twopenny blood suddenly come to startling life. He registered a silent vow that never again would he laugh at a blood. He would never be able to do so, for he would never be able to forget that once he, in company with nine other people, sat bound and gagged in the kitchen of a quiet country house, while in another room were two corpses, one of them the body of a murdered man, and somewhere about the house were four masked foreign spies. A sudden, furious spasm of wind came to remind him that even the elements had entered into it and were, as if by way of doing their bit, putting up a storm of the like seen in this country only in the cinema.

The banging of a door somewhere in the house brought his thoughts around to the four people who had so easily, and with such unruffled calm, trapped and bound them all. Was one of them the murderer? If they had managed to make their way to the house now, they might have done so during the night. But a moment's reflection made Brent doubt this conclusion. Obviously they were all foreigners, and without the faintest shadow of a doubt, what they were after was Manning's formula. Had they come during the night, they would have got it then.

What had probably happened was that they had left the securing of the formula to Strange, and when that individual had failed them, they had taken advantage of the storm to come and get it themselves.

His thoughts went, quite naturally, to a consideration of the formula itself. What Manning had said about the gas he had discovered or made, must then be true, and if this was the case, a child could realise the importance of such a weapon; would understand that the possession and clever use of it would make any country supreme in the world.

A terrifying thought, this. And here was he, a patriotic Englishman, bound helplessly to a chair while such history was being made within yards of him. Even the murder of Manning, the problem of who had committed it sank into insignificance in the face of what was happening then in the house.

Brent wondered what country they had come from, those masked men and that clever woman; how they would get their prize out of the country, and just how quickly the police could act upon such information as they had to give them.

Without doubt they had their preparations thoroughly made; he had seen enough of their efficiency to be quite sure of this, and even such a circumstance as the failure of Strange would have been taken into account by them.

Brent passed the next few minutes in wondering what was going to be the outcome of it all. The four would presumably find what they were searching for. They would probably know exactly how to go about such a search and, of course, they would have the advantage of Alice's acquaintance with the house and its late master's habits to help them. Having found the formula, they would depart, and in the course of time—how much, he did not know, but supposed that this would depend upon the life of the storm—somebody would come and release him and the others in the kitchen. The telephone wires were either cut or damaged by the storm, and this would mean a considerable delay before information could be given to the police head-quarters at Frenting. The police would then, he presumed, have all the ports watched, and do what they could to make it impossible for the formula to leave the country.

But what information could any of them give the police? They could provide a full and accurate description of Alice, and that was all. Strange, who might have helped here, was dead. As far as he—Brent—knew, none of his companions in the kitchen knew anything about the three masked men, and all that he knew in connection with them—and only possible connection at that—was the name of a "Mr. Jenkins" who lived at Frenting.

And that would be all the police would have to go upon in their search for the stolen formula.

Brent estimated miserably that by the time the police had time to act at all, the formula would be safely out of the country and well on its way to the country which it would make supreme in the world.

He strained at the bandages about his wrists, tried to move his shoulders and his legs, but he succeeded only as far as the material with which he was bound stretched under the strain, and that was little enough. Those men certainly knew their job when it came to bonds. He paused for a breather and tried again, but the only result was the wrenching of his right wrist which made him wince with pain.

He looked up and caught Kay's eyes upon him. They were excited eyes this time, full of some message which she was trying to convey to him. But this time, even Kay's eyes were defeated, and Brent saw a little frown of thought appear between them. Then, suddenly, the frown disappeared, and the eyes filled with excitement again.

But, even as they did so, Brent heard a step outside the door which was pushed open, and, one by one, the three masked men, followed by Alice, filed into the room.

Chapter Eighteen

One to Two (Continued)

ALICE, WHO CAME IN LAST, POINTED TO DOCTOR Henderson and said something in the strange language, whereupon the three men approached the doctor. Two of them unbound the bandage about his face and extracted the gag from his mouth, while the leader—"Mr. Jenkins," as Brent mentally dubbed him—took up his position in front of the chair.

"Doctor Henderson," he said in his perfect English, "we are sorry further to trouble you in this manner, but the fact is we have failed to find the combination to the safe, and we cannot spare the time to open it by other means. We believe that you, being a close friend of Mr. Manning's, can help us. Will you be so good?"

The doctor did not at first reply; perhaps because his mouth was dry and stiff from the gag, a fact which one of the three noticed, for he motioned to Alice, said something to her, and she immediately went to the scullery and came back with a glass of water which she held while the doctor sipped it.

"Well, Doctor?"

But the doctor continued silent, and after waiting for some moments, the leader nodded to his colleagues, who thereupon commenced a thorough search of the old man's pockets. Letters, papers, and various odds and ends were taken from them and handed over to the leader who examined them one by one and then dropped them to the floor at his feet; until at last the two searchers indicated with shrugs of the shoulders that the search was at an end.

Through it all the doctor had maintained his silence, and when the leader spoke again his voice contained something a little sinister.

"I feel sure, Doctor, that you will not compel us to make you speak?" he said. "The necessity of having to tie you all up like this is absurd enough without making us add the further absurdity of compulsion—a necessity which would, believe me, grieve us sorely. Please, then, Doctor."

The doctor studied the speaker intently, as if trying to pierce the scarf which covered most of his face.

"What makes you think," he said at last in his gentle voice, "that I know this combination?"

The other shrugged his shoulders and spread his hands in a gesture curiously at odds with his perfect English voice.

"If you will give us your word of honour that you do not know it, we will be content," he replied.

"I can give you that," replied the doctor. "I do, in fact, give you my word of honour that I am not aware of the combination which opens Mr. Manning's safe."

"Nor where we might find it?"

This time the doctor was silent again, and the masked man bent forward eagerly.

"Doctor," he continued, "it will take us perhaps an hour, or little more, to get the safe open. You are not, therefore, preventing us from searching it. We ask you to help us merely to save time."

"Why should I help you?" The doctor's voice was still gentle, and there was no sign of fear in his face.

"There is every reason why you should not," was the reply, "every reason, and you have our complete sympathy in your refusal to do so. But we play for a big stake, and it is a game in which there are no rules. Once more, will you tell us how to open the safe?"

"I am afraid that you must carry out your threat and compel me to do so."

"I am sorry; but I understand. It is the most unpleasant part of our work, and, believe me, we would go to great lengths, were it possible, to avoid incurring the contempt of such a man as you are, Doctor."

He made a little bow, and turned to Alice. The other two joined them, and for some moments there was a whispered conference between them.

Then presently Alice went to Helen's chair and, bending down, removed the slippers from her bare feet. The bound girl slept on, blissfully unaware of what was going on around her.

Alice went into the scullery and returned presently with a candle and a box of matches. Having lit the candle she handed it to the leader who placed it on the floor, making it stand upright by dropping a little hot wax, and placing it upon that. The candle fixed to his satisfaction, the man rose to his feet and confronted the doctor once more.

"A beastly method, Doctor," he said. "I use it only because

it is simple, and because I know quite well that it would be useless to our purpose to attempt any such treatment upon yourself." He motioned to his two companions who, taking up their positions each side of Helen, prepared to grasp her foot.

"A word from you will stop the proceedings immediately," said the leader, turning to Henderson whose face had turned suddenly grey.

For a long moment he studied the eyes above the scarf, and must have read in them the pitiless purpose of the man, for presently he gave in, speaking with a voice which had grown hoarse:

"The safe is opened not by a combination, but by a switch in Mr. Manning's bedroom which is directly over the study," he said.

"And where is this switch?"

"Inside the alarm at the side of the bed. The top of it can be removed."

The masked man turned immediately to the door.

"When you have pressed the switch," the old doctor continued, "the safe is opened by pressing the small button which you will find in the top left-hand corner of its back."

The man bowed, and was about to turn again to the door, when he remembered something. Coming back into the room, he went to Helen's chair, knelt before it, and with his own hands replaced the slipper on the bare foot and removed the burning candle.

"I am exceedingly grateful to you, Doctor," he said as he rose to his feet, "for relieving us of such a loathsome necessity as this." He threw the smoking candle to a far corner of the room, and bestowing another little bow upon the bound figure of the old man, he nodded to the other two men and left the room.

These latter replaced the gag in the doctor's mouth, and then they, followed by Alice, also left the kitchen.

Brent heard them go upstairs. There followed a long period of silence, and then, at last, came the sound of the front door banging. The foreigners had gone, taking with them, no doubt, the formula.

Chapter Nineteen

Two to Three

ONCE MORE SILENCE REIGNED SUPREME IN THE KITCHEN; a silence imposed not only by the gags, but by the horror of the escape of the sleeping Helen, for even Sir Anthony did not make a sound.

Lady Fane and Mary had both fainted, and neither had recovered when the front door banged. Tony's face had gone paler than ever, and his eyes were closed. The old doctor sat with his head bent forward on his breast. He might have been praying. Kay was straining forward in her chair, her eyes fixed upon Brent, who presently looked up and caught her intense gaze.

He remembered as soon as his eyes met hers. She had been trying to convey something to him before the men came in, and he concentrated upon the effort to receive her message.

She nodded to him, and he nodded back, as if to tell her that he knew she had something to "say," and that he was all attention.

She turned her head as far as it would go to her right, and then back to him. Again she turned her head, and Brent, rightly thinking that she was attracting his attention to something in that direction, followed the direction of her head, but saw only the wall at her side and behind her. She repeated the movement several times, each time looking back at him, but he shook his head, and the little frown between Kay's eyes deepened.

For a moment she sat motionless, and then tried again. The same jerk to the right of the head, but this time her eyes were brought into play too, the lids, at first being wide open, and then lowered slowly. Then she looked back at Brent hopefully, but again he shook his head.

Kay tried again. This time, instead of lowering her eyelids, she kept them wide open, and lowered her eyes, and at last Brent understood. He looked at the floor to her right. At first he could see nothing which conveyed anything to him.

There was a distance of perhaps two yards between Kay's chair and the wall on her right, and some three between her and the wall behind her. The corner of the room, which was formed by these two walls, was in shadow, and Brent guessed that it was something in this shadow to which Kay was trying to attract his attention, and he stared into it, straining his eyes to penetrate it.

He saw something at last. It looked like a power point, and—yes, there was something plugged into it. Brent could make out, now, part of what, he felt certain, was a small cable. But where did it lead to? An electric iron, perhaps? Or...? And then he understood. A fire of some sort, of course! What a fool he had been not to spot it before! Kay could only mean that there was a small electric fire of some sort there, and if he could manage to get his bandages up against the wires of that, he could burn them through.

He looked up at Kay again. She was trying to wriggle her body to and fro in her chair, a frown of desperate effort to make him understand, between her expressive eyes.

He nodded, and immediately the frown disappeared, and a smile came into her eyes. Then Brent prepared himself for his effort. What he had to do was, somehow, to upset his chair, and then wriggle his way across to that plug. Once there, he could easily press it down with his head, and if that fire was not tucked away beneath the table which was behind Sir Anthony and the doctor, all would be well—unless, of course, it had one of those wire guards over its front. But even then...

He took a great breath and heaved sideways. The chair creaked, and the sound of it made Kay's eyes dance with excitement. Brent tried again, and this time there was a distinct movement, and the legs grated on the stone floor. One more heave, still more movement, and Brent paused for a breather. The bandages across his chest and about his arms seemed to have become tighter as a result of his efforts. Those men had certainly known how to tie up a man.

A minute's rest, and he tried again, with an upward and sideways movement. The chair lurched distinctly. He must be careful to see to it that when the chair fell, it did so sideways, and not backwards, for, apart from the danger of knocking himself out on the floor should his head strike it first, Brent rightly feared that, once on his back, tied to a chair, he would never be able to get on to his side.

He strained forward as far as his bonds would allow him, and gave another heave, a second, and a third. Each time the chair moved, but the legs never left the ground. He saw that it would have to be done in one great heave. No number of lesser ones would do it.

Brent relaxed for a rest. He had made some half-dozen efforts, and already he was bathed in perspiration. Something in one of the pockets of his waistcoat, probably his watch, was being pressed into his ribs with each heave, and was hurting him badly. The bandages about his wrists, too, seemed to have become as tight again, and his hands felt swollen and painful. He looked up at Kay, and, to his horror, saw her try to heave herself sideways. She, apparently, had the same idea. He shook his head at her, and frowned and glared. She smiled back at him with her eyes, and relaxed in her chair.

Brent concentrated on his next heave. He must pull it off this time at all costs. He strained forward in his chair, gathered his muscles together, and suddenly, as if to take the chair by surprise, wrenched his whole body sideways. The chair lurched. Brent managed a second thrust, and the chair toppled slowly over, balanced itself on two legs for the fraction of a second, and then fell heavily to the ground.

Brent tried to take the fall on his shoulder, but only partially succeeded; for he received a stunning blow on the side of his head, and for two or three minutes he lay where he had fallen, his ears filled with singing noises, and a red mist dancing before his eyes.

Presently the mist cleared away, and he opened his eyes. His head ached badly from the blow, and his shoulder was numb. He tried to move his uppermost arm, and discovered that he could do so with what almost amounted to freedom. The back of the chair had cracked in the fall. Brent found that he could move his left arm quite six inches, and he silently cursed the soundness of the chair. A cheaper one now, he reflected, might have broken up altogether, and by now he would have been free. But the result of his fall was better than he had expected, and he began to try movements with his legs. Here, again, he found that he could move with a little more freedom, and he decided that, the blow on the head and the damaged shoulder notwithstanding, he had much to be thankful for. Now he must try to wriggle his way across to that power point.

He glanced up out of the corners of his eyes at Kay, and found her gazing at him with swimming eyes. As he looked at her, she blinked, and a tear made its way down her cheek.

Kay crying! He had seen her cry before, of course, once or twice, but then she had cried more with anger than anything else. He was certainly seeing quite a new side of his future wife. She opened her eyes again, and he managed a wink. He winked again and again until the smile returned to her eyes, and then he devoted himself to the journey across the floor to her side.

Chapter Twenty

Two to Three (Continued)

IT WAS HALF-PAST TWO WHEN BRENT ARRIVED AT KAY'S chair on his way to the power-plug. The six yards of painful, sweating wriggling had taken exactly twenty-five minutes to achieve—a tribute to the soundness of both the chair and his bonds; a tribute, too, to Brent's powers of endurance, for with every separate effort on the way had come an agonising wrench at his damaged shoulder, and an explosion inside his aching head of such force that he felt sure the top of it must be coming right off.

Two more yards and he would be able to deal with that switch. From where he was he could see, around the back of Kay's chair, that the cable which led from the plug was attached to a small bowl-fire which, he thanked his stars, was not only free from the table, but had no wire guard fitted over its front.

The sight of it heartened him, and raising his head sideways, he winked up at Kay who, her head twisted over her right shoulder, was looking anxiously down on him out of the corners of her eyes.

As he returned her look the sweat trickled off his forehead into his eyes, and thirty precious seconds were lost as he blinked them free of the salty liquid. Then, inch by inch, he struggled on.

Literally, inch by inch; and never before had big Bill Brent, who had once covered a hundred yards in ten seconds, realised how long two of them could be.

Presently his foot brushed against the leg of Kay's chair, and he spurted forwards for six inches with the tiny kick he was able to give it; a great help this, and a saving of nearly two minutes.

He must be getting nearer. He paused and tried to bend his head back far enough to see the plug; but before he could do this he had to wriggle himself into a new position.

He saw it at last. It was not more than a foot away from him, and the nearness of it put new heart into him.

A few more painful wrenches; a little more singing in the ears and thudding in his head; a little more sweat, and he would be there. One—two—three jerks—another, and yet another—one more for luck before he eased up for a second's breather—just one more...

He closed his eyes and dropped his head to the floor. He must have that breather at all costs.

Something round and hard touched his forehead; the cable, of course. That must mean that he was within inches of the plug.

One more jerk then, and—yes, he could feel it now against the top of his head, and all he had to do was to get his head above the switch and press it down.

He wriggled another inch and felt for the switch. It was

there right enough. He pressed on it with his head, felt it give slightly, redoubled the pressure, and then heard it go down with a loud click. So far so good. Now for the fire.

From where he was he could see it easily, and he watched it anxiously for the first reddening of the wires.

Suppose, after all this, there was something wrong with the confounded thing! Just suppose that it wouldn't work, that he had had all this pain and struggling for nothing! It looked old enough; its reflector was dented and battered, and the wires looked as if they were broken in more than one place—and one little break would be enough.

Brent stared at it with burning eyes. Would the damned thing never show a sign?

The sweat ran into his eyes again, and he closed them, pressing the lids hard together to squeeze it out. Then he opened them, and, had his mouth not been gagged, he would have shouted for joy; for the wires were reddening; burning with a steadily increasing brightness.

Brent watched them burn to a bright orange glow, and then concentrated on the next step.

The problem was to get some part of his bandages in contact with that burning cone. This once achieved, freedom would be a matter of only so long as it took for the linen to burn through.

He came to the conclusion that to attempt this with the bandages about his wrists would be to attempt the impossible, for this would mean lying on the bowl, working without the aid of his eyes, and the possibility of breaking the fire itself. The only possible part of his bandages would be, to begin with, those about his ankles, and he set about working himself into position.

More wriggling, more pain, more sweat—much more sweat now, for he had to work in the heat of the fire; and by five minutes to three, his right foot and ankle were touching the bowl. A half-turn on to his knees, and Brent felt the burning heat on his ankle, and smelt the acrid smell of burning cloth.

He twisted his head round until he could see what was happening at the fire. Another inch was needed to get the bandage itself on to the wires, and with a little jerk he thrust himself forwards. Now the bandage itself was exactly in position, and it was a matter of sticking it long enough to allow it to burn through.

It may have taken half a minute; it may have taken an hour. What man can estimate the length of seconds or fractions of seconds of agony? How describe them in terms of time or of anything else?

Brent shut his eyes and bit on his gag, cursing this latter because it got between his teeth and his lip, blessing it because it stopped the groans which he felt rising in his throat.

Came, presently, a short or long—it was all the same to him—period of unconsciousness; a moment when things went suddenly black before him, and his ears filled with the sound of rushing waters. Then another moment when the pain at his foot made him jerk his right leg violently, and a sensation of surprise and bewilderment as he felt it free. One more heave of his body which rolled him over on his back and away from the fire, and he closed his eyes again and breathed deeply.

The pain of his burnt ankle stung him to frantic effort, and he kicked madly against the rung which joined the legs of the chair. In three kicks he had broken it, and in another three the bandages about his left ankle were torn away. He could get to his knees now, and even stand up with his body half-bent.

He staggered round to the middle of the kitchen floor, looking round desperately for something against which he might bang the chair to which he was bound, but there was nothing but the floor, and for the next two minutes the others watched him hurl himself down, struggle to his feet, and hurl himself down again.

Again and again he did this, heedless of the additional pain of bruised limbs, striving frantically to free his hands so that he might touch his burned foot.

And at last the back of the chair gave with a loud crack, and Brent wrenched one hand free, tore at his other bandages, and stood there, free of the chair, swaying on his feet.

His head swam dizzily, the darkness crowded in upon him again, and even as he pulled away the gag from his mouth, he lurched suddenly, and crashed once more to the floor.

But this time he was free; he had two hands with which to clutch his face and keep his head from bursting; a mouth which was free from the gag, and through which a deep groan might make its relieving way.

It was the sound of this groan which pulled Brent back from the onrushing darkness, and gave him the strength to struggle again to his knees, and in another second he had command again, and presently he took his hands away from his face and blinked the mist away from before his eyes.

Then it was that Brent saw something on the floor at his knees; something which lay there among the papers which the masked men had taken from the doctor's pockets, and with a sudden stiffening of his whole body, he stretched forth one trembling hand and picked it up.

It was a photograph; a picture of—surely, Helen? But, no, Helen never did her hair in that old-fashioned way, or wore those old-fashioned clothes. And the other figure? Henderson himself—a younger version of Henderson, Henderson as a young man...

But it was not the portrait itself which made Brent forget for the moment even the pain in his foot; it was the smear of red ink which ran across it; the frayed edges which showed that it had been torn away from something, and which sent Brent's thoughts scuttling back to that moment in the study when he had raised the dead man's head and turned the page in the album.

He raised his head slowly and his eyes met those of the old doctor before whose chair he was kneeling.

For a long moment the two men stared into each other's eyes, and then, presently, the bandaged head of the old man nodded as if in answer to the question in the other's staring eyes.

Chapter Twenty-One

Three to Four

KAY SIGHED WEARILY, AND PASSED A HAND OVER HER EYES. Her head ached and the faint smell of chloroform which hung in the air made her feel sick. Quietly, as if Brent in the bed were asleep and not drugged, she took her hand off his where it lay on the coverlet, rose to her feet and tip-toed to the window which she opened still wider.

The storm was over. When the first excitement of being released had passed, nearly half an hour before, they had all noticed, suddenly, that the wind had dropped as suddenly as it had risen, and that the rain had dwindled from a tropical downpour to a mere drizzle; and now the world outside was strangely quiet, and full of fresh, earthy smells. Kay leaned out of the window and drew in deep breaths. Away to the west a streak of bright light appeared in the still-overcast sky, and from the trees away to the right came the song of a bird. Everything seemed calm and soothed, and even as she gazed at the drenched countryside beneath her, the wet leaves of the trees caught the light from that far-off streak in the western sky and glistened and scintillated.

The house was quiet, as quiet as the world outside. Brent lay there in the bed as still as death but for the regular rise and fall of the sheets over his chest. Kay tip-toed back to the bed and stood looking down on him.

At the bottom of the bed the clothes rose in a little heap, and she shuddered as she looked at this. It was caused by an improvised cradle which the old doctor had fixed up to keep the weight of the bedclothes off the injured foot, and she had helped him arrange it. She, too, had been there in the room while he had dressed and bandaged the injured foot. He had found chloroform in the laboratory, and she had been kept out of the room while Brent had been given it; but only on the understanding that, as soon as he was asleep, she should be allowed in to help. And she had helped, holding up the foot with its hideous burns while the old doctor bandaged it, biting her lips the while to keep down the feeling of nausea which threatened to overwhelm her. And old Hendy—dear old Hendy—had encouraged her with kind words, thanked her with a still kinder smile, and ended up with a pat on the back and a word of praise for her courage before he had left the room to go to Helen who had remained unconscious right throughout the ordeal in the kitchen, and even while she was being carried back to her room.

Mrs. Geraint, too, had had to be attended to, not to mention Lady Fane, for both had collapsed as soon as they had been unbound. Mary, too, had had to be sent to her bed.

Dear old Hendy! What on earth would they have done without him? Brent had unbound him first, and had then done a minor collapse on the floor at his feet, and it had been Hendy who had done the rest; he who had sent Teddy and

Tony off to Maylings for the police, and whatever other help they could get. He, it was, who had seen to the comfort of the three other women, and attended with quick, skilful fingers to the terrible injuries of Brent.

Yesterday seemed a long time ago, a much longer time ago than the twenty-three and a half hours that it really was.

This time yesterday they had all been sitting on the lawns at Fane Court waiting for Tony to return from Treeholme with the result of his visit to Manning. She, Kay, had then been quite convinced that her love for Brent would have to be hidden for ever, and that he would never look upon her with anything but contempt. This time yesterday, she had been what she looked even now with her absurd Eton crop, tinted fingernails, and painted eyebrows. What a fool she had been this time yesterday! What an idiot to persist in, and even to enlarge upon these ridiculous affectations simply because of that first astonished look of amusement and contempt which Brent had given her when first he had come to Fane Court, eighteen months before!

And today, nearly twenty-four hours later, she was a different person, hating the Kay of yesterday, looking forward, with humility almost, to the Kay of the future—the Mrs. Brent to be.

But then, so many things had happened. Manning had been killed, and so had Strange. It came almost as a shock to Kay as she stood at her lover's bedside in the quiet room, to remember suddenly that down below were still the two dead bodies. Then that extraordinary business in the kitchen, the sudden appearance from nowhere of the three masked men, the cruelly tight bandages, and that awful wriggling fight of

Bill's. She shuddered as she thought of this—shuddered for the hundredth time since three o'clock, as she recalled the dull thud of his head and shoulder against the floor when he had first fallen, and that terrible smell of burning behind her as he lay with his foot on the fire. And that desperate, frantic, agonised struggle in the centre of the floor when he dashed himself again and again against it...

Kay shut her eyes and shuddered yet again. She opened them presently and they filled with tears as she looked down on the face of the man beneath her. What a marvellous man he was, this big lover of hers! And what a marvellous thing that he was actually in love with her! She would try her best to live up to him, to make him, as nearly as she could, the wife he deserved.

She leaned over the bed and pressed her lips gently against his forehead. Soon now, they would take him back to Fane Court and she would have him to herself for long days while his foot got better. It would give her a great chance to show him how much he meant to her, how...

Somewhere in the house a clock struck the half-hour. How long, she wondered, would Tony and Teddy be? Three or four hours? It depended, she supposed, on the state of the roads; but in any case, they would not be much longer, and then they could all go away from this dreadful house with its dead bodies...the police, of course! They would be here, and then would begin the business of finding out who really had murdered Manning.

This made her think of Tony, and wonder uneasily if he would repeat his confession to the police before they all came back. Had it, then, really been Helen? Had she, in a moment of fear or frenzy, killed her father? Something she had said had undoubtedly made Tony rush downstairs and blurt out his confession—something she had said in her delirium. What, then, would happen to her? They wouldn't hang her, surely! But they would lock her up somewhere—lock her up for the rest of her life, and then what would Tony do? But perhaps, after all, it was really one of those men who had come after the formula, or Alice. Alice might have done it, for wasn't she one of them? She could, quite easily, have found the opportunity, she had been in the house all the time.

Kay went again to the window. The chloroform in the air upset her. Bill, poor soul, was breathing it out into the air with every breath. What beastly stuff it was! If she didn't get another breath of fresh air she would be sick there and then.

The bright streak in the sky was widening. The top of the little hill away there to her left stood out against it in clear silhouette. The bird in the tree had found others to join him in song, and a gentle little breeze came and shook the leaves of the trees, making them empty the water they held. Kay listened to its soft, pattering fall on the ground beneath. It was going to be a lovely evening with one of those beautiful sunsets.

Somebody opened a window away to her right. She leaned out to try to see which it was, and decided that it must be one of the windows in Helen's room. That was Hendy, then, who opened the window. She continued to lean out and look, hoping that he would lean out too, in which case she would call to him. But he didn't do so, and presently she withdrew into the room. Should she just run along to Helen's room and find out how she was? And have a word with Hendy too at the same time? Bill wouldn't wake for a long time yet. And perhaps she could run downstairs and make a cup of tea for Hendy and her father. The thought of tea raised a familiar yearning within her. She could do with a nice hot, strong cup herself. Yes, she would run along the corridor to Helen's room and put the idea to dear old Hendy.

She dropped another light kiss on Bill's head and tip-toed to the door, opened it softly, and closed it gently behind her. Then she walked swiftly along to Helen's room, opened that, and peeped inside.

There was nobody there; at least, no Hendy, only Helen lying in the bed, still asleep.

Wonderingly Kay looked about the room, and then stepped inside it and tip-toed to the bed. At its side was a small table, and on this a little pile of papers caught her eye, for one of them, the topmost sheet, stirred in the draught of air from the open window and floated to the ground.

Kay stooped and picked it up. It was covered with pencilled writing. Something made her scan the first line, and as she did so, her other hand went up to it and gripped the paper with a convulsive little jerk.

For the first line ran like this:

"I killed Horace Manning."

Chapter Twenty-Two

Three to Four (Continued)

"I KILLED HORACE MANNING."

The words seemed to stand out from the paper in living letters which danced before Kay's eyes as she read them.

> "This will set at rest any further worry on the part of those who have spent the night with me here in this house. I write this for two reasons; because it is right that I should confess, and because the fact that Manning was hopelessly insane might have sorrowful results for my beloved little Helen."

Here the writer had evidently paused, for there was a considerable gap between this line and the next, and there was greater firmness in the writing of the next words than in that of the last few.

> "Yes, Manning was insane. I had suspected it for some time, but I had no definite proof of it until last night

*when I saw him alone in his study. I sought him out
there to talk with him, to ask him what he meant to do
in the matter of Helen's engagement, for I knew that
he intended some evil. I was right. I found him seated
at his table studying his album. Nobody else but he
and I had seen that book of photographs, until yesterday afternoon when, so he told me, he had shown it
to Helen. It was his book of hate; its pictures, most of
them taken by himself, are what he has used all these
years to keep his hatred and bitterness alive.*

"He showed it to me. He showed me, in particular,
one photograph of our darling Helen with Raymond.
But I must tell the story from the beginning.

"Twenty-five years ago my brother and I—my
twin brother—met and loved Helen Mayne. We
loved her, as we had done everything else—together.
All through our lives Raymond and I had lived more
closely together than ordinary brothers ever could. We
liked the same things, thought the same thoughts, we
even knew each what the other was thinking without a
word being spoken. It was natural to us that we should
both fall in love with Helen Mayne, and we loved her
with no bitterness between us. Raymond was almost
grieved for my sake when she chose him instead of me;
though how she could tell us apart was what puzzled
most people who knew us.

"But she chose Raymond, and I was as glad for
him as he was grieved for me. It was wonderful to
think that this beloved woman would belong to one
of us, to my dear brother. It seemed to make up to me

for my loss that I should see them happy together, be with them often throughout their lives, share, as their nearest and dearest friend and relative, their sorrows and joys. This is how Raymond would have felt too, had Helen chosen me.

"But something happened to disturb this happiness. Helen's father lost all his money, and the day came when quite suddenly, she wrote to Raymond telling him that she could not marry him, that she must marry the wealthy and brilliant young Horace Manning. We tried—Raymond tried—to get to her in time to prevent this terrible thing happening, for she was abroad at the time, in South Africa with her father; but before we got there she was already married.

"We came back to England, Raymond to eat his heart out, I to try to comfort him. Then only six months after they had been married there came a cable from Helen begging us to go to her at once. We went, and discovered her terribly changed. Her eyes had filled with fear; she told us that she lived in terror of her husband, that she was afraid that he was mad.

"Manning was that most dreadful and pitiful of mental perverts, a sadist; a man who could torture with a word or a glance. He could, by his very proximity and presence, strike terror and misery to the gentle heart of our beloved Helen. Her father was dead, suddenly, and she was alone in the world. Not, however, that he would have been of any help to her in her *terror; for he was weak and unseeing of the suffering of others.*

"Our poor, beloved Helen! Unhappy, miserable, alone! The sight and thought of her suffering filled our hearts with one single purpose—to free her, to save her from further wretchedness, and even in this we failed her.

"Raymond stole her away from Manning, and he let her go; let her go as a cat will let a doomed mouse wander a few inches away from its claws. It was months before he stretched out his claws to bring her back, and fate played into his hands. He had refused a divorce, and when he found her Raymond had, as he knew, been killed in an accident and a child was coming. He offered to take her back, and she, poor soul, had no choice in her extremity.

"She died, and another Helen—the Helen who sleeps near me as I write—was left. Out of death came another life, another body which was to grow so like the one which had given it birth. Study the photographs in Manning's album to see how like they are.

"Manning gave her his name, registered her in his own name so that, legally, she has always been his child, and only he and I have known the secret truth of her birth. He took the child, of this I feel sure, so that upon her he could wreak the cruelty he would have inflicted upon his dead wife; upon the child he would satisfy the hate of my brother and his wife, and in me he found yet another victim for

his revenge. There were the two of us, so like the two he hated; the child growing each day more like her mother; I the living image of the man who had— so he thought—wronged him. This was why I was allowed, year after year, to be near the little Helen. To me she was a sacred trust from my dead brother and the woman we had both loved. Had he in his death throes given her to me to care for, my mind could not have been clearer on this point. I have said that he and I were of one mind, and, maybe, in the hour of his death his mind and mine were in contact one with the other. And my nearness suited Manning; for he could watch the two of us. He was a cat with two mice to torture and play with; two mice who never knew when he would strike, what would be the nature of his revenge, and to a great extent I was helpless, for there was the secret of the child's birth lying just below the surface of our lives, ready at any moment to thrust its ugly way up into the sight of men to shame her.

"Manning brought the child to England and settled here in this house. I followed them and bought a practice in the village. Here she has grown to beautiful womanhood, and I have grown old watching her, trying as best I could, to give her the love she has missed all her life, trying, too, to keep away the terror which lives behind her eyes. And I have spent many an hour of the night wondering how it was all to end.

"I watched the love spring into life between her and Tony, and it frightened me. How would Manning

regard it? Would he not, most certainly, forge from it a weapon with which to torture her? And how could I be sure of Tony if I told him the secret of her birth. You, Tony, must forgive me for this doubt. I know now, from last night, how true and splendid is your love for her. You faced what you thought was certain death for her, did you not? You will be true to her, of this I am sure.

"And at last that secret must come out. It must be known that she has none of his blood in her, for he was mad, hopelessly, incurably, dreadfully mad. The years of hatred, of secretly nursed revenge, of quiet, unnoticed cruelty, have rotted the weak fabric of his brilliant mind. For, make no mistake about it, Manning was brilliant. All the scientific world knows how brilliant he was. In these last years he has perfected his weapon of death, his poison gas. He has told me of it many a time; I have watched his face and eyes light up with gloating at the thought of the suffering and terror his discovery could bring into the world. It was as if I watched the final yielding of his mind, its last tottering upon the brink of the dark abyss of insanity. And as I watched I knew quite well that to convince others of his madness would be difficult, almost impossible for some time to come. He was an international figure, a name in the great world of science, a giant in the field of research, and soon now, he would have been honoured by his king for his work and achievements. How could I, a simple country doctor, hope successfully to denounce

him to the world as the madman he most certainly was? In a year or two—three at the most—it would have been apparent, and men would have known him for what he was.

"Last night I went to him to face him, to find out what he was going to do to Helen; for I had read some secret purpose in his eyes. You—all of you—saw him during the evening; you were present in his laboratory during that dreadful experiment; but even you would have consented to a verdict of eccentricity, would you not? Only Helen and I knew the truth.

"He told me what he had intended, and his intentions convinced me, who needed no convincing, that his mind was gone completely. His idea was to allow Helen and Tony to marry, and to choose a moment during their honeymoon, a moment during the height of their happiness, for Tony to die horribly. And Helen, having watched him die, was to die herself. It was to be done, so he told me, with his gas which, as he explained to you last night, he could make so that it worked to whatever time he fixed.

"He told me—and this, perhaps, was one of the strong proofs of his madness—where the formula was. But the formula was of little use without a further key; for it was not enough to know the ingredients of this gas which, after all, anybody could find out by analysis. Temperatures of some of the ingredients when they were added, exact quantities, and other like information were necessary. And none of this could be found out without years of research; for with changing

temperatures, with the cooling of the liquid or of the gas, the quantities of the ingredients changed, and the true figures could not, therefore, be discovered by simple analysis. And this key he had concealed in a most extraordinary place. It was written in indelible ink on the back of a photograph of Raymond and Helen's mother, on the photograph which was the centre piece in his book of hate. He showed it to me, and I watched him paste it around the edges and put it back in its position in the album.

"I challenged him, of course. I told him that never, while I was alive, should such a fate come to Helen, and he laughed at me with mad, gloating eyes. I myself, he told me, was doomed; had upon me, where he had sprinkled it during the evening, the terrible death he had invented. I had fourteen hours to live. It was two o'clock then. I am to die at four.

"That clock on the table, Bill. It fell because I pushed it off with my hand. It was an accident, the result of my agitation while he told me of the fate he had prepared for Tony and Helen. But in one sense you were right. Manning did not die at that moment; not physically, anyhow; but in my mind he died, for it must have been just as that clock fell that I decided that he must die.

"I had to leave him to think of a way to kill him. In the drawing-room I found Kay and Teddy asleep, and I watched you two for a moment or so. You, Kay, looked very sweet and womanly in your sleep. May you be happy always! You will, I am sure, for you are *too fine to make bad mistakes, and even your sorrows will be of the kind that you would not be without.*

"I found the knife on the dining-room table and went back with it to the study. I became as cunning as the madman at his table. He was still poring over his book of hate, and I went and stood over him as he turned the pages. He showed me again the centre page where he had pasted the photograph of Raymond and Helen, and he bent low over it as if he would stare his gloating hate into the imaged eyes of the two. It was my chance, and I struck. I struck in the name of pity and mercy; for the happiness of a girl's life, for her unborn children, for the sake of the madman's soul. There was no great hatred in my heart at that moment, this I swear; for Raymond was with me there in the study. I felt his presence around me, and I seemed to know that he approved. Raymond has been with me throughout the day until the storm raised, and now, as I write, he is calling to me. He is outside waiting for me on the top of that hill there. Presently I shall go to him, and he will be with me through the agony of my passing,—my brother, my other self.

"I took the photograph. That formula those men found will be useless to them, and I have destroyed that picture with its terrible secret. I am sure I have done right. There is enough terror, enough suffering in the world without this added horror.

"Bill, you knew I had killed Manning, didn't you? I saw it in your eyes when you picked the photograph

up from the floor, in that moment before you fainted.
I would have told you sooner, but so much happened
afterwards, Strange dying, Helen ill, Mrs. Geraint,
too, and Lady Fane. I have been busy during my last
hours, and I have been glad they have been enough for
me to have been of some service.

"It is past the half-hour. My time is coming nearer
with every tick of the clock.

"Good-bye, Helen, my darling—and yet, not
good-bye, for I am going to join your father and your
mother, and together we will watch over you, guard
you from all evil. When you think of us, think like
that—that we are near to you, as Raymond, your
father, has been near to me all this day. God keep you,
my darling.

"Another twenty minutes. Raymond is calling to
me. I can hear his voice quite clearly. All right, old boy,
I am coming. Just one more kiss on this beloved face,
and I will come to you..."

———

Kay laid the last sheet down. Her eyes, which had followed
with absorbed interest every scribbled word, filled with a
sudden rush of tears, and as she looked about her the room
swam and became a blurred, watery jumble of objects.

She ran to the window. Somewhere out there Hendy was on
his way to his death. She dashed the tears away from her eyes in
order to see the clock on the mantelpiece. Five to four! He had
just five more minutes to live. She must go to him. She must

be with him to help him when he died, to hold his old head in her arms, to let him know that he would not be alone, that…

She rushed from the room and down the stairs. He had said in this letter that it was to the hill that he would go. If she went through the study, she could run straight down to the wood beyond the garden, climb over the fence there. Beyond the wood was the hill.

Without a moment's hesitation she opened the study door, and made her way past the dead body of Manning, stepped over the half-naked corpse of Strange and thrust the French windows open, and in another second she was flying across the grass to the fence. She tumbled over it and dashed through the wood, falling once in her hurry, and bruising her knee. But in a trice she was up again and running almost blindly, the tears falling down her cheeks.

The end of the wood at last, and she paused as she ran out into the open.

There he was, walking steadily up the hill. She would have run after him, but…was she mistaken, or was that somebody walking with him…?

Something, some instinct within her kept her back, made her stand and watch as the figure of the old man went up the side of the little hill.

He breasted the top and stood, a dark silhouette against the lightening sky.

Then suddenly the sun peeped out from behind the heavy, lifting pall of clouds, and sent its first radiance about the old figure, catching the silver hair, and lighting it up like a halo, wrapping him around with welcoming light and warmth.

And it seemed to Kay as she stood and watched with awed eyes and bated breath that once again there was another by the old man's side; one who took his arm and bore him up as he stumbled forward.

The moment passed, and the bent figure seemed to straighten suddenly and walk right into the radiance of the growing sun. It blinded Kay's eyes, so that she could not see.

And back in the study through which she had just come, the clock struck four.

THE END

If you've enjoyed

TWICE ROUND THE CLOCK,

you won't want to miss

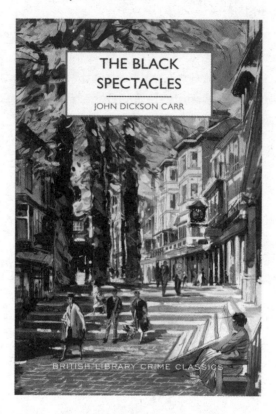

THE BLACK
SPECTACLES

JOHN DICKSON CARR

BRITISH LIBRARY CRIME CLASSICS

the most recent
BRITISH LIBRARY CRIME CLASSIC
published by Poisoned Pen Press,
an imprint of Sourcebooks.

Don't miss these favorite British Library Crime Classics available from Poisoned Pen Press!

Mysteries written during the Golden Age of Detective Fiction, beloved by readers and reviewers

Antidote to Venom
by Freeman Wills Crofts

Bats in the Belfry
by E. C. R. Lorac

*Blood on the Tracks:
Railway Mysteries*
edited by Martin Edwards

Calamity in Kent
by John Rowland

*Christmas Card Crime
and Other Stories*
edited by Martin Edwards

Cornish Coast Murder
by John Bude

Continental Crimes
edited by Martin Edwards

Crimson Snow: Winter Mysteries
edited by Martin Edwards

Death in the Tunnel
by Miles Burton

Death of a Busybody
by George Bellairs

Death on the Riviera
by John Bude

Fell Murder
by E. C. R. Lorac

Incredible Crime
by Lois Austen-Leigh

Miraculous Mysteries
edited by Martin Edwards

Murder at the Manor
edited by Martin Edwards

Murder in the Museum
by John Rowland

Murder of a Lady
by Anthony Wynne

Praise for the
British Library Crime Classics

"Carr is at the top of his game in this taut whodunit... The British Library Crime Classics series has unearthed another worthy golden age puzzle."

—*Publishers Weekly*, STARRED Review,
for *The Lost Gallows*

"A wonderful rediscovery."

—*Booklist*, STARRED Review, for *The Sussex Downs Murder*

"First-rate mystery and an engrossing view into a vanished world."

—*Booklist*, STARRED Review, for *Death of an Airman*

"A cunningly concocted locked-room mystery, a staple of Golden Age detective fiction."

—*Booklist*, STARRED Review, for *Murder of a Lady*

"The book is both utterly of its time and utterly ahead of it."

—*New York Times Book Review* for *The Notting Hill Mystery*

"As with the best of such compilations, readers of classic mysteries will relish discovering unfamiliar authors, along with old favorites such as Arthur Conan Doyle and G.K. Chesterton."

—*Publishers Weekly*, STARRED Review, for *Continental Crimes*

"In this imaginative anthology, Edwards—president of Britain's Detection Club—has gathered together overlooked criminous gems."

—*Washington Post* for *Crimson Snow*

"The degree of suspense Crofts achieves by showing the growing obsession and planning is worthy of Hitchcock. Another first-rate reissue from the British Library Crime Classics series."

—*Booklist*, STARRED Review, for *The 12.30 from Croydon*

"Not only is this a first-rate puzzler, but Crofts's outrage over the financial firm's betrayal of the public trust should resonate with today's readers."

—*Booklist,* STARRED Review, for *Mystery in the Channel*

"This reissue exemplifies the mission of the British Library Crime Classics series in making an outstanding and original mystery accessible to a modern audience."

—*Publishers Weekly*, STARRED Review, for *Excellent Intentions*

"A book to delight every puzzle-suspense enthusiast"

—*New York Times* for *The Colour of Murder*

"Edwards's outstanding third winter-themed anthology showcases uniformly clever and entertaining stories, mostly from lesser known authors, providing further evidence of the editor's expertise…This entry in the British Library Crime Classics series will be a welcome holiday gift for fans of the golden age of detection."

—*Publishers Weekly,* STARRED Review,
for *The Christmas Card Crime and Other Stories*

Poisoned Pen
PRESS

poisonedpenpress.com